Balls and Strikes:
Understanding Tax Liability

Tehrrek Fitzpatrick

D1714937

Copyright © 2022 by IP Publishing
FIRST EDITION
For more information, please contact:
info@ip-publishing.com
Balls and Strikes Website:
www.ballsandstrikesbook.com
ISBN: 9798503822458

Coaches' Commentary

"Tehrrek Fitzpatrick has hit a homerun with Balls and Strikes and he will help YOU hit one too. Having been a top advisor and now coaching top advisors and business professionals in the world, this is a book that is needed during these tumultuous times. Inning by inning instead of chapters, Tehrrek educates you on what is happening in the marketplace, giving you the tools that help you hit a home run with your financial game plan."

—Ben Newman, Performance Coach
Author of Uncommon Leadership

"Balls and Strikes is a whimsical look at a serious topic overlooked by 90 percent of all investors. One of my most valued mentors has always challenged me with "if what you thought to be true, turned out not to be, when would you want to know?" Balls and Strikes helps you methodically work your way through what you have commonly accepted as truth. Tehrrek has done a great job, and you will be challenged to look at what you consider your most valuable asset in an entirely different way."

—Bryan S. Bloom, CPA
Author of Confessions of a CPA: Why What I Was Taught to
Be True Has Turned Out Not to Be True

Dedication

This book is dedicated to all the professionals I have had the pleasure of crossing paths with over the years, and to my parents, who constantly remind me that I can do anything.

In 2018, according to an analysis of 15.8 million participants, Fidelity Investments reported that 157,000 people had one million dollars or more in their Fidelity 401(k) accounts, which amounts to only 1 percent of their 401(k) account holders.[1]

---

[1] Brandon, Emily. "Are Your Retirement Savings Ahead of the Curve?" US News & World Report. November 2020. Accessed May 12, 2021. https://money.usnews.com/money/retirement/401ks/articles/are-your-retirement-savings-ahead-of-the-curve

"It ain't what you don't know that gets you into trouble. It's what you know for sure that just ain't so."

-Mark Twain

Table of Contents

Chapter One

First Inning

Ryan used his index finger and thumb to adjust his tie, the brilliant red standing out against his crisp white shirt. Arming himself with confidence, he glanced at his reflection in the rearview mirror one last time before slipping out of his gray C-Class Mercedes. He rolled his shoulders back, exuding his most fearless stance, as he took in the many levels of floor to ceiling windows that were sprawled out before him.

Drawing in a deep breath, Ryan scanned the bold black logo that was front and center on the main door. The IP Group, with its angled I and P, was an image that he had started memorizing months ago. It was on every document that Ryan had read about the company, from website content to the description of the job that he was vying for. Having been at his last firm, Bail Out Bank, as a 401(k) enrollment specialist, for ten years, he was ready to move on and his confidence in financial industry knowledge led him to this very moment. He held his padfolio tight to his side as he marched toward the front door. Grabbing the oversized silver handle, he pulled the door open and was instantly immersed in a world of wonderment. The building was buzzing with business, and he could practically smell the scent of money as he inhaled another breath to calm the few nerves he had dancing around inside. Having helped customers build their retirement plans for the last ten years, Ryan was certain he'd be able to have a comeback for any question the interviewer threw at him.

Head up, speak slowly, and smile. He repeated the words to himself as he approached the massive white rectangular desk that served as the receptionist's perch.

"Hello, how are you today?" he asked the young girl at the desk. *Always make good eye contact.* He couldn't help but notice how attractive she was. A cascade of brown hair fell to one side as she looked up from a laptop.

"Hi, can I help you?" A glowing white smile peeled across her lips, a contrast to the bright red lipstick she was wearing. She wore red-rimmed glasses and was covered in head-to-toe navy-blue attire.

"I'm Ryan Anderson, I have an interview with Michael James at nine-thirty."

"Yes, of course. Hi, Ryan." The girl scanned him from head to toe taking in his polished appearance. "You can have a seat in the waiting area." She gestured to a circle of white chairs separated by boxy end tables that were the same glowing shade of white. To add to the cutting-edge appearance, iPads were placed perfectly at the center of the tables.

"Thank you." He paused, his gaze searching for a nametag. *During an interview, use names whenever you can.* "I didn't catch your name."

"Amelia." She reached a hand across the desk's shiny surface.

"It's nice to meet you, Amelia." Ryan shook her hand with assertion but not so much that it revealed arrogance.

Two other people were seated in the waiting area. Naturally, he assumed the younger guy sitting on the opposite side of him, swiping a finger across an iPad, was a fellow candidate, his nose for competition sniffing him out. In another seat, an older woman looked up from her phone, offering Ryan a Cheshire Cat grin. He immediately sought her out as the biggest competition, likely the one having the most experience and confidence. Just as he was starting to feel his competitive nature rise, he heard his name.

"Ryan Anderson?" A tall woman stood before the waiting area, scanning her gaze over the three of them.

"That's me!" Overly excited, Ryan jumped to his feet, extending a hand before him, as if he was an elementary school student begging to be called on.

"Nice to meet you, I'm Clara Donahue. I'll be showing you to Mr. James' office." She held an iPad to her chest and led Ryan down a long, expansive hallway before she punched an elevator button that would take them up to the eighteenth floor. It wasn't until he was trailing on her footsteps after they got off the elevator that he realized just how tall she really was. In black ballet flats, the woman was towering over him. As if she wasn't intimidating enough, her hair was pulled back into a neat ponytail, tightening all of her features and wiping away any potential for friendly facial expressions. Her stride, naturally longer than his, made him feel like he was following her like a puppy dog.

Ryan tried to pick up the pace to keep up, but he kept slowing down to take in the magnificent artwork on the walls, the shiny hardwood floors that contrasted with the silver handrails overlooking the lower levels. Sleek glass served as a divider between offices, stairwells, and even the sky. Ryan had been in some impressive offices before but nothing quite like this. He had started to immediately envision himself working in the building. By the time they arrived at Michael James' office door, his shoulders were rolled back, his head high, and he was ready to take on the interview. A wave of the job description passed through his head one last time, as excitement built heat beneath his newly tailored suit. He was prepared to drop all the key words he memorized from the job description, reading them to himself over and over again. *Accumulation, preservation, distribution.* Maybe he would even throw in something about tax analysis for good measure.

Ryan's confidence, not arrogance, was somewhat justified. In addition to his financial prowess, he had an MBA and graduated top of his class at Louisiana State University with incredible offers to Ivy league schools and graduate programs. Ryan, while unassuming, was sneaky smart, a fine combination of intelligence, athletic background, and drive. His friends often joked that he was the guy that nobody wanted to be up against in trivia.

Much to Ryan's surprise, Clara walked through the entryway to Mr. James' office without alerting him. He remembered all the times his current and hopefully soon-to-be-former boss, had urged employees to knock before entering, reprimanding anyone who barged in unannounced

"Hi, Mike, Ryan Anderson is here for his nine-thirty interview."

"Yes, yes…come on in." Mr. James bolted upright from his chair; a backdrop of the Houston skyline framing his slender build thanks to the floor to ceiling glass wall behind him. Before today, it was the type of office that Ryan had only seen in movies. He was quickly beginning to resent his current boss for placing him in a boxy office with carpeted floors and one small window that looked out into the parking lot of a strip mall. How could he ever go back to that, after being in the presence of *this*? This setting was one that he could be highly inspired to work in. Even when he passed a few employees walking from one end of the building to the next, he picked up on the way they all seemed to be in on one big secret. *Was it the secret to success?* Ryan was determined to find out. Mr. James stepped forward from behind the desk and greeted him with a friendly handshake and an even friendlier smile. "It's a pleasure meeting you, Ryan." He gestured to one of the simple black chairs that sat in front of his equally simple black desk. "Take a seat…you can leave my door open, Clara."

"It's so nice meeting you, Mr. James," Ryan said as he slipped into the chair.

"I'm going to stop you right there. Call me Mike. Mr. is for old people."

"Will do, Mike." It had only been seconds since Ryan set foot in Mike's office and he was already absorbed by the man's positive energy. He felt like he could spill his guts to the stranger who was sitting in front of him.

"So, Ryan, how did you find out about us?"

"To be honest, Mr. James–Mike, I've been searching for something different. Quite honestly, I've been looking for more of a challenge," Ryan said as he thought about the unorthodox job description he had memorized. "I heard about your group from a friend of mine and–"

"What did you hear?" Mike tilted his head, getting right to the point and offering his undivided attention.

"Well, I just heard that you guys are really successful and forward-thinking and with my experience and background, I'm sure I'd be a good fit here." *Use the keywords.* "I've had a lot of success helping clients build quality retirement plans and I feel like my resume paired with my drive would be an asset to this company." The words spilled from Ryan's lips and his confidence and experience began to break through. He felt as if he was nailing a presentation that he had been rehearsing.

"Well, I'm glad word is spreading about our group. You are correct; we have a very unorthodox approach to what some call *financial planning*. Our team here at The IP Group is forward-thinking and they know how to speak for themselves." Mike paused for a moment, setting his gaze on his hands which were interlaced on the desk. "We believe education is key and with education, we create a lot of confidence. I have to be honest, I'm quite impressed with your resume. It's obvious that education is very important to you." Mike rocked back, resting his forearms on the arms of the chair, as if he was in a casual conversation. "Let me ask you a question."

Ryan nodded, eager to hear what Mike had to ask him.

"When was the last time you felt very strongly about something?"

A smile washed over his face. This was an easy question. Having always considered himself as someone who had a very black and white approach to life, he had the perfect answer.

"Actually, a strong opinion is required in my second line of work." Ryan smiled at his own joke. "You see, I umpire college baseball. Naturally, I feel strongly about the game, about the rules, and about the calls that I make. And it goes without saying that some may disagree with those calls. I imagine you've been to some games?"

Mike nodded as Ryan continued. "The strike zone is a judgment call and now that I think about it, a strike zone is entirely an opinion." Ryan used his hands to convey his passion for the topic, a habit he had been doing since he was a young baseball player himself. "I've been challenged by some very close calls, and I've had no choice but to stand my ground, to follow through with what I believe is right." He let out a gruff chuckle. "Trust me, I've been called a boatload of names while umpiring. It's not rare for me to be accused of being blind or having a bad eye."

Mike's lips tilted upward into a grin, emitting a smile of understanding. He could appreciate Ryan's love for the game.

"Did you ever play any sports?" Ryan inquired.

"Actually, I played a lot of ice hockey in my day. I do love a Friday night baseball game though. There's something so relaxing about the cool air, the lights, and a cold beer." He leaned back in his chair, assessing Ryan in a way he hadn't before. Kindness peeled up at the corners of his eyes, and Ryan couldn't help but feel that they had formed a slight bond over sports.

"I've been to my fair share of hockey games as well. I don't envy those refs one bit. Calling hockey games makes baseball look like a walk in the park...no pun intended."

The two shared a laugh. Ryan's comfort was inflating by the second. He managed to delve further than the average interview questions and into other parts of his life. Some would say that it was too soon in the interview process, but he couldn't help but feel that the two of them had found some common ground. After a small pause, Mike casually asked, "How good are you with numbers?" A genuine, thoughtful look presented itself on his face.

Quick to respond to the dramatic shift in conversation, Ryan said, "I'm a math person. I see the world in numbers. What did you have in mind?"

"Humor me for a moment, will you?"

"Of course." Ryan shifted in his chair and put his game face on as Mike continued.

"Everything we do here is entrenched in math, facts, and data. Math is what gives us our strength, power, and confidence. It's our competitive advantage. I want to know if you have the ability." He shot another inquisitive look in Ryan's direction, in full-on interview mode.

"Your background." Mike held up a piece of paper, scanning his eyes across the black print. "I see you have a lot of experience as a 401(k) enrollment specialist at one of the largest 401(k) providers in the industry. I also see you were servicing the largest oil and gas companies here in Houston, and you dabbled in project management," Mike recited the resume.

"That's correct." Ryan nodded.

"I'm going to ask you a loaded question," Mike said with a sly grin. "If on the day your client retires, he has $2,000,000 in his 401(k)...how much money does he have?"

Ryan took a deep breath, sensing it was a trick question.

"Well, that depends. How are their assets allocated and what percentage of stocks and bonds do they have? What's their risk tolerance?"

Mike fired back in attorney mode, "Irrelevant counselor, but I'll stipulate. Let's say you are in a balanced portfolio with a low risk tolerance, then how much money do you have?"

Ryan shot back an answer that seemed obvious to him. "You have $2,000,000 plus three to 4 percent interest per year."

"That's a great answer, but I'm going to have to challenge that call." Mike paused as Ryan received the proverbial punch to the gut. "I believe the client has a little over $1,000,000."

Ryan was puzzled, and for a moment he wondered if he was being filmed for a candid camera show. He knew he was right; this was a simple question; how could his answer be wrong?

Mike swiped through his phone. "Are you free on Friday at four o'clock? I'd like you to roll that around a bit and get back to me." He picked up a pen and rolled it between his fingers. "Don't sweat it, Ryan, no one gets it right the first time and you and I aren't done here."

Ryan, still working the problem in his head, answered, "Yes, I'll be here." He knew that he'd need to juggle some things on his personal calendar since Friday he was on call to umpire, but his overly competitive nature was urging him to find the right answer and contest the man that was sitting in front of him.

Mike shot up from his chair, his height towering over Ryan's five-foot-ten frame. He then extended a hand, offering another firm grip. His stare seared into Ryan's eyes as if he was testing him, giving him the ultimate challenge. To search for an answer and bring it back to him.

***

As Ryan pushed his way through the main entrance of the building, he watched the angled I and P break apart, a symbol of how he was feeling after the interview. He had gone in with confidence, certain that he would be able to wow Mike with his financial know-how. Instead, he had left feeling bamboozled. He was being asked to come back with an answer to a question that he thought had been so clear-cut and simple, but he was wrong. To himself, he admitted that he was flustered but at the same time he was inspired. He knew exactly who he would take the math problem to.

He slid his phone out of his pocket as he sat behind the steering wheel in his car, nearly jumping up at the sun-blazed leather.

"What's up?" The familiar voice of his oldest childhood friend penetrated his ear.

"Hey, girl, any chance you can meet me for a drink? I have a math question for you." He heard the sound of her fingers hitting the keyboard.

"Ahhh my two favorite things…drinks and math. Sure, when are you thinking–Bethany, can you contact Dean Domenico and let him know he's all set for the year?" Ryan laughed out loud, thinking about the many conversations that went like this. Maggie Rayburn was always juggling multiple things at one time. She was what one would call a "mover and a shaker" in the CPA world. He always wondered how she had managed to get so much accomplished at such a young age. By the time the woman was thirty, she was head of her own CPA firm, managing major corporations, and some of the top names in Houston. And while she was confident, success never went to her head, and she could always be counted on to meet her oldest friend for a drink.

"How's tonight at five?"

"Perfect, meet me at The Daily just in time for happy hour specials."

Ryan laughed, knowing how much Maggie liked to score a deal. She wasn't a millionaire because she was born into a wealthy family. She got her top-notch education on a scholarship, and she'd worked her way through school. The woman knew how to save, and she knew how to work hard.

Appendix One

The Journey

Welcome to the illustrational portion of the chapter. For educational purposes, I will attempt to display the math, logic, and reasoning behind our main character's journey. You will find some of the math and assumptions are argumentative and designed to get you thinking. You will also find some of the math and assumptions to be precise and educational.

The charts and graphs at the end of each chapter may be different than the numbers referred to in the chapter. The idea is for you to be exposed to multiple scenarios to gain a solid understanding of each chapter.

The appendices will begin at the end of chapter two.

Chapter Two

Second Inning

By the time five rolled around, Ryan felt like his mind had run a mental marathon. Throughout his regular workday, he went over the numbers in his head repeatedly, trying to find the trick in Mike's question. Having credited himself as a financially savvy person, he was stumped, and his confusion was starting to boil into frustration.

When he pushed through the doors of The Daily, the bar had already picked up speed, filling up with workers winding down for the day, likely venting about their last eight hours in the office. Ryan scanned the bar, before his gaze landed on Maggie. As always, her head was down, and she was swiping across an iPad with a well-manicured finger. The woman was always working. Their similar work ethic was one of the reasons why they never amounted to anything more than just friends. The one time they experimented with a relationship, they ended up laughing in the end, as the combination of their highly competitive workaholic personalities didn't allow for any give and take. They were better off as friends, and in some sense, Ryan looked at Maggie as a mentor.

Their friendship didn't stop him from appreciating her beauty, and he was filled with a wave of admiration when she looked up from her iPad. Her green-eyed gaze landed right on him as she welcomed him with a bright smile. Ryan took three long strides, and he was embracing his old friend, comforted by the scent of his youth.

"I took the liberty of ordering for you." Maggie winked at Ryan as the young bartender approached the high top and delicately placed a dirty martini in front of each of them, a favorite pastime from their early twenties when they were making their way through college. The taste of olives always reminded Ryan of late-night talks with Maggie and the many times he was her punching bag when she was venting about a boyfriend.

"Cheers." Ryan lifted the stem of the glass, delicately tapping hers over the table.

"So, what's up, bud?"

He explained the interview, from the breathtaking views behind Mike's desk to the frustration he felt when he was leaving the building. He then presented her with the same question that he had been faced with just hours before.

"If on the day of retirement, your client has $2,000,000 in their 401(k) account, how much money do they have?" The words came out slow and steady, like he was standing in front of a classroom of students learning math for the first time. Part of that was for his own benefit, as he was still baffled by the question, even after he had repeated it to himself at least thirty times.

Maggie took a sip of her martini. Her eyebrows scrunched together, meeting up in the middle like one long fuzzy caterpillar. Ryan could see that she was assessing it for trick-question potential.

"I'm thinking he has $2,000,000 plus interest?" Maggie's response came out laced in a question, well aware that it couldn't be that easy of an answer.

"My thoughts exactly, but when I responded with that answer in the interview, he said that it's closer to $1,000,000." Ryan paused, receiving the look of clarity that was spreading over Maggie's face. "I'm a finance guy, Mags. It's black and white. How could that answer possibly be wrong? It just makes sense. If my client has a balance of two million dollars in their 401(k) account on the day they retire, then they obviously have that $2,000,000 plus interest, which I estimated at three to 4 percent every single year." Ryan flattened his hand sideways making a chopping motion on the table, as he rattled off the rest. "If we stick to the safe withdrawal rate, which is typically a 4 percent rate of distribution from the account balance, then my client would likely get eighty thousand dollars per year from the distribution. It's a no-brainer. Four percent of $2,000,000 is $80,000." Ryan paused to take a sip of his martini before he smacked both palms on the table. "Even if we cut it down to 2 percent, then that's $40,000 per year, which is obviously in addition to $2,000,000. And *even* if they lost 25 percent on the balance one year, it would drop the account balance down to $1,500,000 and they'd be getting 4 percent off that, which would be $60,000. So, how on earth is he getting about a million as the answer?"

"Hold on a second." Maggie's eyes formed into CPA laser focus, eyebrows scrunched together, a lightbulb turning on in her head. "You said this was a 401(k), right?"

"Yeah."

"I think I know our answer."

Appendix Two

Let's Start Thinking

A large portion of what is on your 401(k) statement does not belong to you. If you believe taxes will be higher in the future, then an even larger portion of your 401(k) does NOT belong to you.

401(k) Statement	$2,000,000
Less taxes @ 37%	$740,000
Net After Tax	$1,260,000

$ 740,000 (the amount of your
401(k) that is not yours)

Yes, I know that most people don't liquidate their account all at once. Yes, I know that a flat tax bracket is used in the example instead of a marginal tax.

Let's look at a scenario if you had $2,000,000 in your 401(k) and you liquidated it at $200,000 for ten years. That would reduce your tax rate as shown in the box below.

Annual Liquidation	$200,000
Less taxes @ 32%	$64,000
Net After Tax	$136,000

$64,000 x 10 years (the amount of
your 401(k) that is not yours)

These withdrawal scenarios make some arguable assumptions. Whatever assumptions *you* make, be sure to include the tax liability associated with this type of account. If you recall from the statistics at the beginning of the book, regarding 401(k) balances with an account balance over $1,000,000, the largest assumption being made by these two charts is that you will have close to $2,000,000. Remember, there is less than 1 percent chance you will have more than *$1,000,000*. [2]Having less money in the account does not negate the tax liability.

---

[2] Ibid.

Chapter Three

Third Inning

Ryan pulled his red tie off the rearview mirror, its silky material uncoiling like a snake. As he wrapped it around his neck, crossing the wide end of the red shiny cloth over the thin side, Maggie's words filled his head. "Think about it, when you are dealing with a 401(k), you owe income tax on every single dollar you withdraw," Maggie had said, right before the two had cracked the code on his homework question. He now understood why a 401(k) account holder would lose a little less than half of the remaining amount upon retirement.

Making a final loop, Ryan secured his tie with one expert hand. He prepped his padfolio, pulling out any items that wouldn't be necessary for his second meeting with Mike. Tossing out a baseball magazine, he watched as it landed on the umpire mask that was face-up on the floor of the passenger seat, its pages splayed out like a handheld fan. A pile of his shin guards still encrusted with clay from last night's baseball game, lay beside it.

Over the years, Ryan had grown so confident in his calls during games that he had perfected a steely glazed-over look when he was questioned about them, knowing that he was brimming with undying certainty. He thought he had that same assurance in finance up until Mike stumped him with the question about the 401(k). It had been such a simple answer. All his training had taught him that 401(k) plans were a tax savings and a tax deduction. He knew that they were often referred to as a tax advantaged account, so how could it have slipped his mind so easily that taxes are owed on every dollar withdrawn? If he forgot about that when he worked in the industry and was immersed in it every single day, then what did that say for the average 401(k) account holder? How many of those having a 401(k) simply forgot about the ridiculous amount of taxes still owed on their balances when they were fantasizing about a retirement filled with dollar signs?

This time, as he pushed his way through The IP Group's main doors, he was eager to learn what else Mike had to share with him. Several workers wearing mostly navy blue, zigzagged their way through the lobby, their shadows trailing behind them on the polished white floor that made the entryway look even more expansive than he had remembered.

"Ryan Anderson here to see Michael James."

A girl with shoulder-length strawberry blonde hair looked up from an iPad that she seemed to be analyzing. She greeted Ryan with a puzzled stare before a wave of recognition flashed across her face.

"Oh my gosh, I'm sorry. It's my first day. I'm trying to learn everything at once and you caught me off guard." Embarrassment made itself evident in the red splotches that dotted her pale cheeks.

"No need to apologize, I'm sorry I interrupted you when you were in such deep thought."

"Apparently, I can't juggle more than one thing at a time," she laughed at herself.

"No worries…is Amelia no longer here?"

"Oh, no, she's still here. It's just that she's the lead receptionist and is dealing with some important stuff so you've got me…Lucy… newly hired and at your service." She tucked a strand of hair behind her ear, revealing a simple diamond earring. "So, as you said, you're here to see Mr. James. Let me pull up his calendar." She used an index finger to swipe across the iPad screen.

"Ryan!" A booming voice echoed across the lobby, followed by Michael James himself. He strolled toward the front desk in an easygoing manner as other employees passed by him, greeting him along the way. "You feel like grabbing a bite while we chat?"

Ryan couldn't tell Mike he had just eaten an entire sub at Jimmy John's, hoping to stave off any distracting hunger pangs during his second meeting with the financial guru. "Sure, that sounds good," he responded coolly.

"Great. Sometimes I like an early dinner, especially since I don't eat lunch."

"Sounds good to me." Ryan nonchalantly looked at his watch. It was nearing four o' clock, closer to the time he typically ate lunch, but who was he to turn down an opportunity to dine with the man who could potentially be his future boss. He would have to get through this interview, share the new homework answer he had, and hopefully move on to another interview.

The two walked in step as they made their way out the doors. It was Friday and the sidewalks of the business district were bustling with well-dressed employees. A group of twenty-somethings passed by, their loosened ties evidence that they had punched out for the day and were ready for happy hour. Ryan reflected on when he was that age, just starting out at the oil and gas company and green, a newcomer in the industry. He had come a long way in the field, learning from various mentors and transforming into a well-respected mentor himself.

As they walked, Ryan felt both enlightened and frustrated. He had spent years telling people about what certain portfolio allocations could do for their future. He'd told individuals and employees about target date funds and index funds; he'd listened to 401(k) providers and wholesalers come in and tell him about the latest and greatest mutual funds. He'd run countless models and projections on the 401(k) calculators that he was taught to use so he could show people just how much money they would have in retirement. If he was being honest with himself, he enjoyed studying the market and running hypotheticals, but he was nervous. For the first time in his life, he realized he had never explained to a client that he or she was actually creating a tax liability, rather than a positive fiscal future.

"So, tell me about yourself, Ryan." Mike's voice interrupted his thoughts.

"Well, so I did that math," he responded, eager to get into it.

"I don't mean that, I mean something personal. What do you like to do in your free time?"

"Oh, okay," Ryan paused, not prepared to answer questions about his personal life. He had rehearsed everything about what he would say regarding his homework, but nothing about what he did in his spare time.

"Baseball. Baseball pretty much takes up all my time outside of work."

"Have you always been a baseball fan?"

"Always," Ryan said, as he swerved around a group of older men who looked like they were beyond the age of retirement.

Mike made a quick right turn and suddenly the two of them were standing in front of a glass door with a gold handle. Ryan recognized the sign on the aqua waterfall that cascaded down a gold-trimmed glass wall. Mastro's Steakhouse was one of the best steakhouses in the city and while Ryan had been there a handful of times, he was never there at this hour. It was always for a late dinner, the only time he could get a reservation. Again, he was baffled by the four o' clock start time, considering they typically opened at five. Even at the early hour, several high-end cars were lined up in the valet queue, like a parade of pageant contestants ready to be sized up. A sleek yellow Lamborghini was parked in front of a glowing white one, the two cars decorating the entrance of the restaurant.

"Good afternoon–evening, Mr. James." A man wearing all black swung the door open with impeccable timing, as if he had been watching them approach.

"Hi, Benjamin, how are you?"

"Wonderful. Your usual table today?"

"That would be great." Ryan followed the two men to a table parallel to a short glass wall that greeted an indoor waterfall. The illuminated colors and the sound of the moving water created a relaxing environment that bolstered Ryan's comfort level. *I could get used to this.*

Just as they slid into the seats, a well-dressed man seemed to come from nowhere, and stood with a welcoming grin in front of their table.

"Nick!" Mike presented the man with a widespread smile.

"Mike, welcome back, good to see you, my friend." The man gripped Mike's shoulder and gave him a friendly shake.

"Ryan, this is the legendary general manager, Nick."

"Nice to meet you Nick...you run quite the place here." Ryan's eyes expanded, showing how impressed he was by the posh atmosphere, the professionalism that was ingrained in every staff member he'd seen so far.

"Always a pleasure meeting a colleague of Mike's." Nick winked and turned on a heel, passing by an approaching server. The word *colleague* didn't go unnoticed on Ryan, and he hoped it was a forecast of what was yet to come.

The server set down two goblet glasses brimming with iced water and a dish of freshly sliced lemons.

"Hi, Mr. James. Would you like to hear this evening's specials?"

Mike nodded in Ryan's direction, encouraging the server to move forward in reciting the specials for his fellow diner.

As Ryan tried to follow the server's long list of precise ingredients, he allowed his eyes to scan the dining room. The restaurant, which was massive in size, was occupied by only the two of them and a few staff members that were flitting about. A girl with a tightly fastened topknot polished glasses behind a shiny bar. A rainbow of liquor bottles lined the mirrored shelves behind her, creating a colorful background to the dark brown leather seats that framed the black bar top. Ryan wondered just how connected Mike was, being able to pull off a reservation during the hour before the city's most sought-after steakhouse was even open. He felt like they were having a private dinner.

After the server recited the specials, she turned toward Mike.

"The usual, Mr. James?"

"Yes, please. Ryan, do you need a few minutes?" Mike tilted his head toward his dinner guest.

"Actually, I think I know what I'll have."

The server turned toward Ryan, her eyes wide like saucers, awaiting his request.

"I'll have the ribeye."

"Good choice." She winked at Ryan and turned on a heel.

"Two great minds think alike." Mike angled himself slightly sideways, as he crossed his leg. "The ribeye has always been my go-to choice."

"At a place like this you kinda have to, right?"

"Great point," Mike said.

"My dad got me hooked on the ribeye; it was always his favorite. A medium-rare ribeye is what he and I would get to celebrate a big win when I was younger. In fact, it's what we still do today."

"Did you have a good relationship with your dad?"

"I did. Still do. Dad still comes to a lot of the games that I umpire."

"There is something to be said about a good father-son relationship."

As Ryan was taking a sip of his water, Mike jumped right in. "Okay, so *now* let's talk about my question. Did you have time to think about it?"

Ryan's gaze landed on Mike's, holding his stare much in the same way he did when he was commanding baseball games. "I found out where I was wrong. I failed to take taxes into consideration. When you are dealing with a 401(k), you owe income tax on every single dollar you withdraw, therefore, the value of a person's 401(k) will be heavily dependent on what tax bracket they are in when they retire." Maintaining eye contact with Mike, Ryan continued. "So, I'd like to resubmit my answer and say the account holder will have the amount in their 401(k) net of taxes when they retire, and that will be largely determined by the tax liability that surrounds it."

Mike's face radiated with a smile that reached his eyes. "Base hit!" He rang out his approval just as the server approached the table and set a plate of shrimp cocktail between the two of them. Four generous shrimp reached out from the center of a glass; their tails curled over the edges like fingers extending from the ghost-like dry ice that was emitting from the display. The server delivered her next lines, as if on cue.

"Can I get you something besides water, Mr. James?"

"Yes, I'll have a dirty martini."

Ryan smiled at Mike as the server turned toward him. "That's my go-to drink."

"Two dirty martinis it is." Mike raised his water glass as if toasting, before he took one long sip and set the glass back down. "Is shrimp cocktail also one of your go-to's?" he asked as he plucked a shrimp from the glass.

"It's definitely up there on my list of food choices." Ryan followed Mike's lead and pulled a colossal shrimp from the glass. He reveled in the taste of the shrimp as he watched the server at the bar as she shook and poured their martinis in the same refined mannerisms she used to deliver them to the table. After he took a moment to survey the contents of the glass, he led his train of thought back to the topic at hand.

"Honestly, I can't believe I forgot about the taxes."

"Believe it or not, most people do. That is why the 401(k) is such a failed means of building for a fiscally sound retirement."

"Then why do so many people opt for it?" Answering his own question, he continued. "I mean it is free money after all, isn't it?" Ryan took his first sip of the martini, the questions burning inside him right along with the liquor. He looked down into the glass at the swirling liquid and the stabbed olives sunken like a shipwrecked boat.

"Well, to be direct, Ryan, people opt for it because it's pushed or sold by guys like you, and other financial advisors. You push people into it because companies and 401(k) providers pay you to do just that." Mike paused, taking a sip of his martini. "Surely, you've told people to put as much money as they can into their 401(k), right?"

Ryan found himself nodding, staying silent as he maintained eye contact and taking in every word as Mike continued to speak animatedly about the topic. Even when the server removed the empty shrimp cocktail dish and set the ribeyes in front of them, Ryan kept his stare on Mike, absorbing all the information the man had to offer. Once Mike stopped to ready his fork and knife for his meal, Ryan finally looked down at the display in front of him. A ribeye cooked to perfection sat nestled beside a nest of mouthwatering sautéed onions, both drizzling with butter.

"If you don't mind me asking, did you ever discuss the future tax liability while telling someone to *max out* their 401(k)? Was that ever brought up with any of the employees?"

"No," Ryan answered directly.

Mike shifted in his seat. "I'll be honest, as a financial advisor it makes me sick that people are told to *max out* contributions to IRAs and 401(k)s. They are told it will be a tax savings instead of being told the truth. That it will be a *tax liability*. The financial industry tells people to do that so we can eventually get those assets under management or *roll over* their account when they change jobs or retire. And in turn, we can charge them fees, or as I like to call it...*rent*." Mike shook his head with disgust, just as the server approached the table, checking in but careful not to interrupt the conversation. It was obvious to Ryan this was not their first exchange. "You see, Ryan, the majority of compensation that financial advisors make, comes from assets under management fees." He carefully unfolded the white linen napkin and laid it on his lap, as he gave a nod of approval in the server's direction. "So, if I tell someone to put as much money into a 401(k) as possible, I am doing so because someday I hope you will park that money with me, and I can charge you a percentage to *manage it*." Mike threw up a set of finger quotes as he said the word 'manage.' "Advisors rarely tell clients the whole story about how every dollar that is withdrawn from their 401(k) triggers ordinary income tax, and if they do, they usually tell them they'll be in a lower income tax bracket, which could be misleading."

Ryan was immediately reminded of so many of the firms and other advisors he had met during his time in the industry and how they only talked about the size of their *book*. Right away, he knew Mike was right and that so much of the industry was centered around parking money and charging people rent or fees to have it *managed*. As he cut into his ribeye, the grease and butter wafted up from the plate and into his nose, stimulating his hunger again.

"I hope you don't mind me being direct, Ryan, but I believe people need to know the truth." Mike stabbed at a buttery chunk of onion and continued talking. "And for your second question, it is most certainly not *free money*." A big smile swept across Mike's face. "I've read the 1978 Revenue Act which created tax qualified accounts such as the 401(k) and I don't believe the word *free* is anywhere in that piece of legislation." He let out a hearty laugh. "In fact, the IRS actually calls it *deferred compensation*. In other words, your contributions are not tax savings and your employer's *match* is not *free money*. To the IRS, it's actually compensation owed to you. Now, take that a step further." Mike paused, as Ryan kept a laser focus on his every word while enjoying savory bites off his plate. "Do all companies match a 401(k)?"

"No."

"Exactly. Can companies choose to match whenever or however they feel like it?"

"I never thought of that, but they *can* choose to match or not to match. You're right." With an enlightened expression on his face, Ryan leaned back in his chair.

"Exactly. So, if a company has a bad year, they can choose not to give compensation."

"Holy smokes, that's right!" Ryan said, trying not to use profanity in a job interview.

"Now, take this one step further. How do you get this deferred compensation when it's totally at the discretion of the employer?" Mike answered his own question without pausing. "You actually have to give up some of the actual compensation you're currently earning, to possibly get *optional* compensation. In other words, you need to put your money into the game to be eligible even though your employer doesn't have to contribute if they don't want to. And think about this, if the IRS considers the match your deferred compensation, it doesn't seem really fair that the company can pull that match any time they want, does it?"

Mike finished his martini. With lifted eyebrows he set the glass back down. "We're gonna need shots if we go down this path."

Ryan laughed. But it was hitting him, and as he had a habit of doing, he recapped. "So, let me get this straight. I give up my actual compensation, say 6 percent of my income goes into a 401(k) account in the hopes that my company is actually profitable enough to *match*." Ryan threw up a set of finger quotes around his last word. "*But* my company doesn't have to if they don't want to."

Mike adjusted his posture, sitting up taller. "Correct. But leave out the word profitable. You're giving up your money today in the hopes that they will match if they *feel like it*."

Ryan's face was marked with disbelief and frustration. He finished his martini. "You're right, we might need shots."

"You want the kicker? You'll get a laugh out of this one. Have you ever heard about the guy who created the 401(k)?" Mike leaned forward on the table, getting closer to Ryan like he was about to tell a big secret.

"He was publicly cited for regretting ever having created it in the first place. He actually said he was sorry for having helped open the door for Wall Street to increase the funds they were already making."[3]

Ryan looked around, as if searching for his next words. "Wait, so the actual creator of the 401(k) regrets starting it?" Ryan leaned forward, positioning his elbows on the table outside his near-empty plate, just as the server came by and effortlessly slid both of their dishes away.

"Dessert, Mr. James?"

Mike looked over at Ryan, silently reiterating the question.

"Oh no, not for me. Thank you though."

"I think we are all set." Mike passed a wide grin over to the server before carrying on.

"Yes, the man who actually created the 401(k) admitted to regretting it, and why shouldn't he? Think about it. Congress controls the tax liability you owe on your 401(k), therefore you are putting your financial future into the hands of a potentially irresponsible government. Does that make you feel confident about your future?"

Just as the server was approaching the table with the bill, Mike slid his credit card out of the wallet that was in the inner pocket of

---

[3] Jeremy Olshan, "The Inventor of the 401(k) says he created a 'monster,'" Market Watch, September 2016, accessed May 5, 2021, https://www.marketwatch.com/story/the-inventor-of-the-401k-says-he-created-a-monster-2016-05-16

his navy blue jacket. He handed it over to her along with a wink. "Thanks, Kelly."

***

By the time Mike and Ryan exited Mastro's Steakhouse, it was nearing six. Ryan was buzzing from all the new information he was connecting, as if a lightbulb had been turned on in his brain. The sidewalks were busier than before, as more people were officially punched out for the day and headed to dinner reservations that started at what Ryan thought was a more normal hour.

"If you don't mind me asking, Ryan, how much were you making when you entered the workforce right after college?" Mike walked with a steady stride as he talked.

Ryan's brown eyes moved back and forth, searching for the answer. It was nearly twelve years ago when he started his job at the oil company as a 401(k) enrollment specialist.

"Forty thousand." He couldn't imagine living off that now.

"Okay. And how much do you make now?" Mike looked over at him as they walked side by side in the direction of The IP Group's office.

"Over $100,000.

"Okay, and would you like to see that amount go up in the future?"

"Yeah, of course," Ryan said, the answer simple and obvious.

"Do you know anyone who would say the opposite, anyone who would prefer to make less as they gain more experience in the workplace?"

"Can't say I do," Ryan laughed, as he thought about his circle of friends. Maggie was always looking to jump up in pay, working hard for every extra penny. And the handful of financial advisor friends he had were all equipped with the determination needed to make more money. It kind of went hand in hand with the industry. Or any industry for that matter.

"So, in other words, you'd agree that you have the *ability* and the *desire* to make more money in the future?" Before Ryan could answer, Mike continued with his thought. "Something that I like to call *income potential*."

"Definitely."

"Okay, let's just say you started working today making $40,000. Do you know what tax bracket you would be in?"

"I would guess it would be rather low. I'd say about the 12th percent effective tax rate." Ryan used a hand and smoothed it over his chin, his go-to thinking gesture.

"Okay, and how old are you now?"

"Just turned thirty-five last week."

"Ha!" Mike's eyes expanded as he let out a loud laugh. "Another common thread between us. I turned forty last week." Without missing a beat, Mike continued walking as he led them back to the IP office parking lot.

"Happy birthday." Ryan laughed. He smiled with admiration, learning that Mike was only a few years older than him. Michael James already had a bustling business that seemed to be growing by the second, and here Ryan was just starting to branch off into greener pastures in the financial industry.

"So, by the time you–*we* hit the retirement age, do you suspect you'll be in a higher tax bracket?" Mike stopped walking when they were directly in front of Ryan's car.

"I certainly hope so."

"Okay, so let me ask you a question. Would you knowingly tell someone to defer their income from a 12 percent tax bracket to a potentially much higher tax bracket when they're ready to retire?" Mike smiled.

At first Ryan was puzzled, then he realized that the guy had him, he knew that Mike was right. Ryan silently asked himself, was he making substantially less income right out of college and deferring money into his 401(k) so that it could be taxed at a later and higher tax rate.

"Ryan, you mentioned earlier that you were looking for a challenge and I like how you came back ready to rock with your homework and ready to tackle any question I threw your way. So, with that said, I have another assignment for you." He paused, waiting for Ryan to nod in agreement that he was ready to take on another challenge. "What tax bracket will you be in when you're ready to use that tax liability of yours?" Mike asked. "I'm sorry, I meant your 401(k)." He threw up a pair of finger quotes and accentuated his words, poking fun at the 401(k) before he smoothed a hand on the roof of the Mercedes. "Are you free next Wednesday at noon?"

"I will be."

"Great, I'll expect your answer then." Mike started to walk away and was stopped in his tracks by Ryan's next question.

"Wait–how did you know this was my car?"

"Baseball bat over the trunk. It's a dead giveaway, my friend. You wear that sport like a badge of honor." He saluted Ryan with two fingers angled at his brow line. Ryan turned around and saw the Louisville Slugger that had been a fixture on the back deck of his car, beneath the rear window. The famous font peered up at Ryan, the bold black outline circling the trademarked name of the professionally used bat. *Louisville Slugger.* It was in its designated place, and while it rolled front to back on the deck when Ryan accelerated and braked, the logo always landed face-up for all to see.

Once again, Ryan was standing speechless in the parking lot of The IP Group. The Houston heat had caused a river of sweat to trickle down the back of his shirt. As he slid into the driver's seat, he unfastened the tie from around his neck and hung it back on the rearview mirror. He could feel his phone vibrating in the front pocket of his bag. While he had felt it buzz off and on since he sat down at the table, he'd ignored it, having been so entranced by his conversation with Mike and not wanting to look rude checking it in the middle of dinner.

While reaching for his phone, Ryan started to feel uneasy. He felt ashamed for all the years he spent pushing his clients to *max out* their 401(k)s without any education on the fiscal downfall that could occur. Everyone should put as much money in their 401(k) as possible, Ryan recalled from the training program he was in. He thought and recalled vividly, telling everyone to max out and put as much money into their 401(k) plans. He paused, hit by a thought. *Boy, there is nothing fair and balanced in the way I've been trained.* As he tapped his phone to life, he saw what all the buzzing had been about. Maggie had left a train of messages, just minutes apart.

Balls and Strikes:

I've been thinking a lot about this whole 401(k) thing, and I did some math. We need to meet!

OMG it's all in the math, Ryan! How have we missed this?

Are you free this weekend?

Do you feel like I'm stalking you yet?

I forgot you were in your meeting with the hotshot financial guy. Call when you are done. We have lots to review.

Appendix Three

Let's Start Educating

Providers do not supply you with a 401(k) for free. Instead, they make money in several ways from these accounts, one of which is the "fee" that comes off the balance. If you Google "average 401(k) cost," you will find that a variety of different charges may impact your account balance. These price tags include investment fees, expense ratios, sales loads, or deposit costs, monthly or annual plan administration costs, record-keeping costs, accounting and legal costs, trustee costs, service fees, as well as any other charges a provider may dream up.

Below, we simulate 1.25 percent in total fees. As you can see, this generates $461,898 in fees over the *Accumulation Phase* of the account. You will notice that the $461,898 lost in fees costs you over $1,000,000, the difference between your gross and net balance. This loss is due to the compounding effect of those fees over time. Take a moment and multiply this amount by the number of people that work at your company. For example, if five hundred employees are enrolled in your company 401(k), $230,000,000 would be generated over time. If I were a provider, I would tell everyone to "max out" a 401(k) as well.

Keep in mind that the "fees" can continue during the *Distribution Phase* of this asset as well. Also, you will not get a *Flat Return* of 7 percent every single year. I will simulate some volatility in an upcoming appendix. As referenced in this chapter, you will owe taxes on the balance of the traditional 401(k).

Balls and Strikes:

Age	Contribution	Growth Rate	Gross Balance	Annual "Fees"1.25%	Net Balance
30	$19,600.00	7%	$20,972.00	$262.15	$20,709.85
31	$19,600.00	7%	$43,412.04	$542.65	$42,588.89
32	$19,600.00	7%	$67,422.88	$842.79	$65,699.33
33	$19,600.00	7%	$93,114.48	$1,163.93	$90,106.35
34	$19,600.00	7%	$120,604.50	$1,507.56	$115,878.23
35	$19,600.00	7%	$150,018.81	$1,875.24	$143,086.48
36	$19,600.00	7%	$181,492.13	$2,268.65	$171,805.88
37	$19,600.00	7%	$215,168.58	$2,689.61	$202,114.68
38	$19,600.00	7%	$251,202.38	$3,140.03	$234,094.68
39	$19,600.00	7%	$289,758.55	$3,621.98	$267,831.33
40	$19,600.00	7%	$331,013.64	$4,137.67	$303,413.85
41	$19,600.00	7%	$375,156.60	$4,689.46	$340,935.36
42	$19,600.00	7%	$422,389.56	$5,279.87	$380,492.97
43	$19,600.00	7%	$472,928.83	$5,911.61	$422,187.86
44	$19,600.00	7%	$527,005.85	$6,587.57	$466,125.44
45	$19,600.00	7%	$584,868.26	$7,310.85	$512,415.37
46	$19,600.00	7%	$646,781.04	$8,084.76	$561,171.68
47	$19,600.00	7%	$713,027.71	$8,912.85	$612,512.85
48	$19,600.00	7%	$783,911.65	$9,798.90	$666,561.86
49	$19,600.00	7%	$859,757.46	$10,746.97	$723,446.22
50	$19,600.00	7%	$940,912.49	$11,761.41	$783,298.05
51	$19,600.00	7%	$1,027,748.36	$12,846.85	$846,254.06
52	$19,600.00	7%	$1,120,662.75	$14,008.28	$912,455.55
53	$19,600.00	7%	$1,220,081.14	$15,251.01	$982,048.43
54	$19,600.00	7%	$1,326,458.82	$16,580.74	$1,055,183.08
55	$19,600.00	7%	$1,440,282.94	$18,003.54	$1,132,014.36
56	$19,600.00	7%	$1,562,074.74	$19,525.93	$1,212,701.43
57	$19,600.00	7%	$1,692,391.97	$21,154.90	$1,297,407.64
58	$19,600.00	7%	$1,831,831.41	$22,897.89	$1,386,300.28
59	$19,600.00	7%	$1,981,031.61	$24,762.90	$1,479,550.40
60	$19,600.00	7%	$2,140,675.82	$26,758.45	$1,577,332.48
61	$19,600.00	7%	$2,311,495.13	$28,893.69	$1,679,824.07
62	$19,600.00	7%	$2,494,271.79	$31,178.40	$1,787,205.35
63	$19,600.00	7%	$2,689,842.82	$33,623.04	$1,899,658.69
64	$19,600.00	7%	$2,899,103.81	$36,238.80	$2,017,368.00
65	$19,600.00	7%	$3,123,013.08	$39,037.66	$2,140,518.10
				$461,898.57	

Chapter Four

Fourth Inning

"When you want something, you certainly go after it." Ryan spoke into the hands-free speaker as he made his way out of The IP Group parking lot and onto the main strip. Maggie had picked up the phone after half a ring.

"I take it you got my text messages."

"All five of them." Ryan didn't hide the sarcasm that had a tendency to naturally spill into his personality.

"I can't stop thinking about this, Ry, it's literally kept me up all night with my calculator."

"How is that different than any other night, Mags?" Ryan teased her. "But in all honesty, I know how you feel. I just had my second meeting with Michael James and guess what?"

"What?"

"I have another homework assignment and I need to report back to him next Wednesday."

"Dang, this guy certainly isn't handing the job over to you, is he?" Maggie paused. "I like his style though. So, dinner at my place this weekend? I'll cook."

"How about Saturday night?"

"I guess that means I'll have to get behind the stove, *once again*." Maggie faked stress with a long, drawn-out sigh.

On the handful of occasions that Maggie cooked, it was her go-to spaghetti and meatball dish, with gobs of butter. She didn't have a domestic bone in her body, but she could dominate a calculator like no one else.

"Spaghetti and meatballs for dinner it is." Ryan laughed.

One of the many things he liked about Maggie was the mutual understanding in all their conversations. They never messed around with small talk, and instead got right to the point. Much in the same way that Ryan viewed life, Maggie also looked at things as black and white, open or closed, right or wrong. It was why they both relied on math for nearly everything, whether it was a personal situation or work-related. As Ryan thought about the many late-night conversations he had with Maggie over the years, he was bombarded with memories. One of their other friends, Aaron, was an art major and the three of them would get into major battles over whether math or art was more valuable to everyday life. It was always Maggie and Ryan on one side, both refusing to admit that art had any daily worth. Poor Aaron would always end up cornered, defending the many famous artists that came before him. "When you create or engage in art, you naturally improve stress, which can benefit all aspects of your life," Aaron would argue. Ryan and Maggie would have no part of it and would always list the examples of math used in everyday life. "You can't travel, go to the grocery store, cook, or save money without using some form of math," they would rant, their voices getting louder with each sip of martini.

And now, here they were, putting math back into an equation that they thought they'd known for so long. They were reestablishing the math problem that they had assumed was right when it came to 401(k)s. Ryan was well aware of all that was involved in the progressive tax system. He knew that people with higher taxable incomes were subject to higher federal income tax rates and vice versa for those with lower taxable incomes. And he certainly knew that the government was in charge of deciding on how much employees had to pay based on the tax bracket they fell under, which was why it was easy for him to remember his bracket from when he was first starting out, making only $40,000. What he failed to recognize was the large amount of taxes he would owe when he retired, if he was in a higher tax bracket. And considering how driven he was, he was certain that his future tax bracket would be far higher than the one he was in today. Based on how he saw it jump from when he was only making $40,000 all those years ago, he had no doubt his future would be brimming with taxes.

***

All weekend long Ryan's thoughts had been laced with flashes of his conversation with Mike. The term *income potential* was batting around in his head like a butterfly, flitting in and out of his thinking as he went about various activities. While umpiring a game, he found himself silently examining the income potential of the parents and coaches in the stands. He had recognized many of them and had gotten pretty familiar with them over the years. There was no doubt that these coaches had certainly been climbing the income potential ladder. He wondered about the salary increases when a coach jumped from the high school level to a junior college level. And then making an even bigger leap from there, to a coaching position at a four-year institution.

He thought about the other umpires as well. Most umpires worked a full-time job in addition to their baseball responsibilities. Not only did the umpires work full time but many of their spouses did as well. He recalled the situation his good buddy Ken was in. Ken was an umpire, a full-time teacher and a coach at the school. He was also married to a teacher who was a coach. Ryan let the thoughts swirl around in his head, estimating that teachers made around $50,000, and those that were also coaches, likely made an additional $20,000, jumping their pay up to $70,000 annually. As a college umpire, Ken may make another $50,000. The combination of Ken's and his wife's salaries had to be at least $190,000. Ryan had to remind himself that Ken and his wife most certainly didn't start out at that income level as two teachers right out of college.

He couldn't help but dissect the various examples of income potential that surrounded him on a daily basis. He had recently caught a game with a former fraternity brother who had started his career at a global oil and gas company. He recalled the two of them comparing their starting salaries right out of college. And while Ryan was making $40,000 out of college, Tim had started out at $30,000 plus commission. Pausing to do the math in his head, Ryan calculated what Tim's income would likely be today. With confidence, he concluded that his frat brother's income had dramatically increased over the years and now he likely earned over $200,000 annually in base salary plus sales commission. So, what tax bracket was he in now? As Ryan went about his weekend, he made a special note folder on his phone, annotating all the of discussion points he would bring up with Maggie during their meeting on Saturday.

Appendix Four

Do You Have Income Potential?

I have inserted a copy of the current tax brackets from IRS.gov. Please take a moment to track your ***Income Potential*** and ask yourself the following questions:

- What was your first income from your very first career?
- What is your current income?
- What would you like your income, or your household income, to be at age sixty-five?

2021 Federal Income Tax Brackets and Rates for Single Filers, Married Couples Filing Jointly, and Heads of Households			
Rate	For Single Individuals	For Married Individuals Filing Joint Returns	For Heads of Households
10%	Up to $9,950	Up to $19,000	Up to $14,200
12%	$9,951 to $40,525	$19,001 to $81,050	$14,201 to $54,200
22%	$40,526 to $86,375	$81,051 to $172, 750	$54,201 to $86,350
24%	$86,376 to $164,925	$172,751 to $329,850	$86,351 to $164,900
32%	$164,926 to $209,425	$329,851 to $418,850	$164,901 to $209,400
35%	$209,426 to $523,600	$418,851 to $628,300	$209,401 to $523,600
37%	Over $523,600	Over $628,300	Over $523, 600
Source: Internal Revenue Service (IRS)			

Example of Income Potential for Single Filers and/or Head of Households		
Age	Income	Tax Rate
28 (past age)	$40,000 (past income)	12%
40(current age)	$150,000 (current income)	24%
60 (future age)	$300,000 (future income goal)	35%

Depending on your ambition, industry, or marriage, you may have *Income Potential*. We'll discuss this further in chapter five.

Chapter Five

Fifth Inning

Just as Ryan's index finger was about to greet Maggie's doorbell, the knob twisted, and the door swung wide open. Maggie was dressed like a weekend college student, in a pair of baggy gray Texas A & M sweatpants and a fitted maroon T-shirt. A mountain of hair was piled on her head in a messy topknot with a few loose strands escaping out the back.

"Are you psychic or something?"

"Nope, I've recently just upgraded to a doorbell camera. As soon as this puppy detects motion on my front step, my phone alerts me." Maggie proudly held up her newly enhanced iPhone, with its shiny teal and white case.

"I'm glad you got dressed up for me," Ryan teased as he presented her with a bottle of Cabernet.

"Shut it. I had a late night with the girls out in the city. It started out with a single drink with Addy, and the next thing I knew we were grinding to the Spice Girls on the dance floor."

"Sounds like a typical night with Addy."

"Hey, she's fun. You missed your chance with her." Maggie's gaze was pulled to the wine label, before it jumped back up to Ryan. "By the way, Aaron's in the living room." She turned on a heel and led them through the long hallway that spilled out into a colossal open-concept kitchen. A white granite island speckled with black and gray, took up the majority of the room, complete with a gas stovetop and wine racks installed on each side. When Maggie was in the midst of renovating her condo, Ryan repeatedly questioned her insistence on having such a spacious countertop, considering she seldom cooked.

"You know I hate tight spaces and I love to spread things out so even if I'm eating a microwave dinner every night, I want to be able to have plenty of room to enjoy it, "she had said, when he inquired about her obsession with an oversized kitchen island.

Ryan stepped over the threshold into the living room to see Aaron flipping through a magazine as if he was waiting to be called into an appointment. "Hey, bud, good to see you." He leaned down and the two bumped fists in a natural greeting they had done so many times before. "Did Maggie drag you into our big tax discussion tonight?"

"Nope, she just promised me dinner." He reached over for a glass of wine that was sitting on the side table and rose from the low leather chair. "I had no idea we were talking taxes." An obvious eye roll spread across his face. "Lucky me."

The smell of garlic, butter and tomato sauce broke through Ryan's senses.

"Wow, it smells delicious. Did you hire a chef to come in and cook?" he joked, as the two men walked into the kitchen.

"I will have you know this is all my creation, thank you very much." Maggie stared at the laptop screen that sat inches from the stove. "I decided to venture out from my traditional recipe and throw in some extra spices." She hefted a bowl filled with a concoction of ingredients and poured it into a sauce mix that was simmering on the stovetop.

"Fancy–shall I?" Ryan started to reach for the wine bottle he brought. Maggie had set it on the countertop in her hurry to get back to the pots and pans that were strewn about.

"Actually, we had a little head start. There is an open bottle of Cab in the fridge."

"True Maggie fashion." Ryan winked in her direction as he slid a wine glass off the rack. As he pulled the refrigerator door open on his mission to retrieve the opened bottle, he saw stacks of prepared meals lining the shelves, all boasting of organic ingredients and convenient prep times. He had no doubt Maggie spent many dinners solo at her kitchen island eating these quick meals as she worked well into the night. He poured himself a hefty glass before plopping down onto one of the barstools surrounding the island. Beside him, Aaron looked down at his phone, tapping rapidly on the screen. Although he was an artist and had hippy views on life, Ryan noticed he relied on technology for everything.

"Okay, I think I just have to let this rest for a bit." Maggie put the lid on one of the pans and took a sip of her wine.

"Do you mean simmer?"

"Yeah, whatever." She waved him off as she moved toward the end of the island and hefted herself up onto a barstool. A heap of paperwork sat in front of her, papers piled high and jutting out in various sections where they were tabbed with fluorescent index stickers.

"Whatchya got there?"

"Well, you asked, and I answered. And I may have killed a tree in the process." Maggie slapped a hand on the pile. "You know how I get with my printouts."

Ryan remembered her obsession with paper copies in college. When everyone else was starting to utilize online resources and emailing assignments to their teachers, Maggie couldn't let go of a good old-fashioned printout. During one of their late-night conversations, she had detailed every single thing that she loved about a hardcopy and the security she felt when she had a piece of paper to refer to.

"I'm pretty sure you killed *several* trees in the process," Ryan scoffed.

Ignoring him, Maggie used a finger to flip through the pile, until she found a bright yellow tab labeled *Income Potential.*

"I can't stop thinking about this." She separated a chunk of documents out from the rest and set them on the countertop.

"Same here." Ryan took a sip of wine and leaned forward on his elbows, surveying the print. "It affects everyone. *Nearly everyone,* yet people are still maxing out their 401(k)s, relying on the faith they have in a very old and warped system."

"Exactly. It's like when people first discovered cigarettes were bad." Maggie rested her elbows on the stack of paperwork. "It took a long, long time for it to sink into their heads. I mean, think about how obvious it is to our generation that cigarettes kill you. We've seen it firsthand in our older relatives. Remember when my Uncle Don died of lung disease?"

"Or when my Aunt Carol continued to smoke a pack a day after she was diagnosed with lung cancer. Yeah, I see your point."

"Well, I'm pretty sure that's what we're dealing with here. It's just a different kind of death, like financial suicide." A buzzing on Maggie's watch triggered her to check on the food. She stood up, stirred the meat sauce and bent forward, inhaling the scent of the meat that was now dancing on the hot pan. Flipping the stove off, she went to work dishing out three heaping piles of pasta onto flat white plates, followed up by a hearty meat sauce. Ryan's taste buds came to life as he watched the sauce slide down the mound of pasta.

Looking up from his phone, Aaron chimed in. "What are you guys talking about?"

"Income potential and taxes," Ryan said as another eye roll made its way across Aaron's face. Ignoring his friend's irritation, Ryan continued. "Let me ask you two quick questions, Aaron."

Aaron nodded as skepticism tugged his eyebrows up. He pulled the plate of pasta closer to him after Maggie slid it across the island in his direction.

"Do you want your income to go up or down in the future?"

Without a second thought, Aaron responded, "Up of course."

"Okay, and where do you think taxes will go in the future?" Ryan pressed ahead, as he twirled the spaghetti ropes around his fork. When he was satisfied with the thickness of his work, he crammed it into his mouth.

"Well, even I know that taxes have to go up in the future based on the deficit this country is running."

Maggie and Ryan looked at each other from across the island and their response came out at the same time. "Exactly." They both smiled before they simultaneously speared another hunk of food with their individual forks.

"I've been thinking a lot about this over the weekend. And I concluded one major thing across the board." Ryan held up his fork in a stabbing motion, using it to emphasize his words.

"What's that?" Maggie asked as she wiped at a smudge of sauce that was escaping her mouth.

"We–financial professionals like myself–cannot keep telling people to max out their 401(k)s." His voice got louder and sterner as his fork penetrated the air. "We cannot keep telling people to max out their 401(k)s and we cannot keep telling people they're gonna retire in a lower tax bracket." He turned toward Aaron. "How much were you making out of college?"

"Geez, like $20,000 a year. Not to mention the college debt I had."

"And how is your career going now?" Ryan knew Aaron had worked his way up and was the director of the graphic design department at an advertising firm. He also knew that his friend had a 401(k).

"A little over six figures."

"Congrats, dude, that's awesome. Let me ask you this–if you made it to the top, about how much money would you be making?"

Aaron replied, "You mean like twenty years from now? I don't know, I'd say maybe a few hundred thousand."

Ryan looked at Maggie. "Bingo!"

With a confused expression plastered on his face, Aaron asked, "What am I missing?"

"You're participating in your company's 401(k) plan, right?"

"Yeah, I'm maxing it out and getting a very small company match I think."

Sliding into full-on tax mode, Ryan leaned further forward on the counter, his shirt barely missing a collision with the sauce on his plate. "This is exactly what we're talking about, Aaron, and you just confirmed that. Hear me out for a second." Ryan sat upright, again slicing his fork across the air passionately as he spoke. "Maggie and I have been discussing income potential. You were making $20,000 a year when you first started, yet you're hoping that over the years you'll make closer to a few hundred thousand." Aaron stared at him, keeping up with the numbers, as a dollop of sauce threatened to drip down his lower lip.

As Aaron nodded along and Ryan continued to talk, Maggie took a break from eating to refill their emptying wine glasses.

"Keep following," Ryan said as he held up an index finger. "So, you took money from the lowest tax bracket and now you're deferring it to a point in time when you hope you're making an annual salary of $300,000, at which point, taxes, you believe, will be much higher than they are today."

"Yeah, that seems backwards," Aaron said, matter-of-factly. "So, why are we doing this?"

All three of them laughed.

"Probably because some kid came around your office and told you to max it out."

Without missing a beat Aaron said, "Yep, he comes around every year and tells me to put more money in. And for the record, it's not doing very well."

Following another round of laughter, Ryan got the conversation back on the train tracks, after he used his fork to lift the remaining piece of meat, leaving behind an orange stain on the white plate.

"I would like to think that nearly everyone has income potential, either by ambition, industry, or marriage. I think people generally hope to make more money in the future."

"So, that means that everyone, *nearly everyone*, will likely have to pay a boatload of taxes just as they are about to settle into what they always envisioned as a cushy retirement," Maggie said as she pushed her finished plate away and let out a satisfied sigh. She adjusted the elastic that was barely holding her wobbly topknot in place, before she took several tiny sips of the wine.

"Pretty much–according to the math." Ryan paused, took a big sip of wine, peering at them over the glass before he set it back down. "Think about it, Mags," Ryan said. "Think about where you started and where you are today."

"It's hard to not think about it," she responded. "I see the college loans in the mail every month. I can't believe I managed to survive on such little income while paying those hefty loans when I first started. Kids fresh outta college can only defer loans for what–"

"Six months typically, unless they have some extenuating circumstances."

"I was not one of those kids. I was only making $55,000 when I first graduated, and I was at one of the biggest firms in the city. And that was with overtime and burning the midnight oil nearly every night. I maxed out when the 401(k) rep told me to max out. I did what all the new hires were doing...what *everyone* was doing."

"Same here, sister." Aaron held up his glass in a cheers gesture, and took a long sip.

"You mean what everyone *still is* doing, guys." Ryan felt his skin growing red as frustration lingered within. "The more I think about this, the angrier I get. It's as if we are working and living simply to pay the IRS." He paused, his eyes growing big like balloons inflating with air. "How is that fair?"

"That's the question of the day." Maggie pushed her lower lip out allowing a deep upward exhale. A few flyaway hairs danced on her forehead, accentuating her eyes. Even after a late night, no makeup and sweatpants, Ryan thought she was beautiful. For a brief couple of seconds, he let go of his upset over the 401(k) situation and allowed himself to take in her allure, knowing he *could* never and *would* never act on his attraction to her. He forced himself to focus on something else, even if that meant his anger would be elevated.

"So, Mags, let me ask you this...how much do you make now?"

Without missing a beat, Maggie rolled her eyes. "A hell of a lot more than I was making when I started at that firm twelve years ago."

"Ballpark."

"You mean you haven't salary dot commed me yet?"

"That site is never accurate and you know that," Ryan shot back. "Not to mention the fact that you deal with Houston's finest, so that's an additional thing to take into consideration."

"A little less than a quarter million," Maggie blurted out, proud of the honest living she made from solid, hard work.

Ryan whistled, insinuating his applause for her noteworthy salary. He had, in fact, salary dot commed her but the number she shared was higher than what was reflected on the calculators the site used. Almost immediately his mind circled back to the calculators that the 401(k) companies used to determine how much an employee would *allegedly* have upon retirement.

"Long hours, risk, sacrifice, focus and dedication is what landed me that salary number."

"I don't doubt it, which brings me to our next point."

"What's that?" Maggie asked. Aaron's eyes darted between the two financial gurus, now fully invested in the conversation.

"Those salary.com calculators are about as accurate as the 401(k) calculators."

"Not denying that. According to the figure I got when I salary dot commed you, you only make $55,000." Maggie raised an eyebrow and let out a quick giggle.

"You might want to stop laughing…you're not too far off."

"Eek. For real?"

"$70,000."

Without hesitation, Maggie asked, "What would your dream salary be?"

"I'd love to be in the 400k range."

"Do you think you have that type of potential if you land the gig at The IP Group?"

"I certainly hope so."

"So, Ry, if you land that gig and your income potential is 400k, how much do you think you'll be paying in taxes when you retire in say, twenty-five years?" Maggie repeated the question they had been pondering in a sarcastic manner, but they were both thinking the same thing. It was a legit question that every single person with a 401(k) should be asking.

"Touché." Ryan spotted one of the yellow index tabs titled *stale money* and slid out the bundle of paper that had been stapled together. "What's this one all about?"

"Oh *that* gem is about *stale money*," Maggie said with a sarcastic smile.

"When you roll money over and don't consistently add any money to it," Ryan said as if he was answering a question on a pop quiz.

"Bingo! And guess who has a lot of stale money that will be subject to taxes upon retirement?"

A question mark formed between Aaron's eyebrows, as he tried to keep up pace with the other two.

Ryan gave her a puzzled look, waiting for her to gift him with the answer.

"You're looking at her." Maggie formed two thumbs-up symbols with her hands and aimed them toward her chest. "Remember back when I was making only 55k at the firm right out of college?"

"Yeah."

"Well, I did as I was told by the rep who signed me up for my qualified account, and I *maxed out*." Maggie held up a pair of finger quotes, hugging the now forbidden term. "But then I changed jobs which means that I have an old rollover IRA just sitting there. I'm adding to my new 401(k) and no one told me to add money to the old one. In fact, I haven't heard from the guy at the bank who set up that IRA in years. Now get this…I recently looked at my statement and the balance hasn't changed at all. And I bet that guy at the bank is charging me a hefty fee."

"Hmmm." Ryan flipped through her IRA statements and realized she was right. The balance hadn't change in about five years. He recognized she had gone through some significant losses and the balances never recovered, which he concluded as the very definition of *stale money*.

Ryan summed up the situation. "Just within this room we have Aaron with income potential that could hammer his retirement with future taxes. Maggie, you have a pile of *stale money* that isn't doing well sitting in an IRA, which will also get pummeled with taxes." The three of them looked at each other, before Ryan shook his head as he transitioned into another thought. He took a long gulp of wine, looking down at the empty glass again. Without hesitation, Maggie, retrieved a bottle opener from a drawer beside the deep curtain sink and went to work opening another bottle. She maneuvered her arms, navigating her way around the empty plates as she filled the glasses, this time to the brim, with a Zinfandel.

"Dude, it's like a cruel punishment for years of hard work," Aaron concluded.

"I see this every day, Ry, and I don't know why I've been so blinded by it." Maggie looked down at her glass, suddenly recognizing the ridiculously full pour. "Half of my clientele are lawyers who started out as junior associates at law firms. Since then, they've moved on to partner, and they've paid their homes off." And with a partner-level income and paid-off assets that means they have less deductions and more money owed to the IRS."

"Damn, this tax thing just gets worse the more we think about it," Aaron said, officially intrigued by the topic.

Ryan adjusted his posture and read the document titled *Average Top Tax Brackets.* [4]"So, according to this table, it appears that the average top tax brackets are 60 percent. If you average the top tax brackets over the last one hundred years, you will get 60 percent. A 60 percent average top tax bracket…unbelievable." He used an index finger to guide him as he read the next part. "And according to this, if your income grows at 3 percent, and taxes work their way back to the alleged averages, the value of your taxable portfolio goes down drastically."

"Hearing that read out loud makes me even more mad than when I read it eight times to myself." Maggie's eyebrows crinkled together, forming an enraged expression that Ryan didn't even think she was capable of. Having a natural baby face, Maggie usually had trouble showing upset through her facial expressions. Her round eyes decreased in size until they were two angry slits, her full red lips pursed together in one fat straight line and her posture stood erect, as if she was ready to take on the tax Gods.

"Reading it out loud makes me downright angry," Ryan said. "So, these people, meaning *us* and all of our friends, our parents, relatives, and colleagues, are making more money every year, paying off more assets, which could cause them to lose their deductions, and in turn they could end up in the highest tax brackets, with lower deductions when they retire." Ryan paused, dropped the paper on the island, feeling heavy from both his newly expanded belly and the weighty conversation. "Am I understanding that correctly?"

---

[4] https://www.irs.gov/statistics/soi-tax-stats-individual-tax-statistics

"Yep, and that is why I believe your newfound mentor, Michael James, is onto something seriously legit."

Reading each other's minds, Ryan and Aaron rose from the table and started cleaning up the dishes.

"I'm drying," Aaron said as he reached for a towel that was hanging on a hook just above the sink.

"That meal was phenomenal by the way," Ryan said as he made soapy circles on a pan with a pink sponge.

"What can I say, I'm a master at spaghetti."

Aaron expertly dried a pot, weaving the towel between the handles and shimmying it left to right. "You know what's scarier than Ryan complimenting you on your food?"

Maggie and Ryan looked over at Aaron expectantly.

"The lethal combo of rising taxes and income potential." He paused, setting the pot on the counter. "If my income keeps growing in the direction I want it to, won't I climb the continuously increasing tax brackets, making the value of my 401(k) even less?"

"Oh my God Art Major, you're right," Maggie joked. "If those two things happen simultaneously, you're screwed." A double whammy! Income potential and increasing tax brackets, both working against you!" She paused, as all three of them linked eye contact. "You know what this calls for?"

"What?" Both Aaron's and Ryan's brows transformed into two question marks as they awaited her next move.

"You know!" Maggie reached for her phone, held it up, showing off the iTunes display. She pressed play and just like that, Ryan was taken back to the past. The lyrics to *The Pina Colada Song*, filled the room and they were back in their glory days, pre-gaming in college before a night out on the town or at one of the many fraternities they frequented. Long before Maggie's cheeks had thinned out and Ryan lost the fifteen pounds he had gained from eating microwave dinners nearly every night. Having liquid courage, Ryan swayed side to side showing off what little dance moves he had, as Maggie threw away all her inhibitions and belted out the lyrics, shifting her body into a series of grinds and spins. Aaron raised his arms in the air, showcasing his go-to move from the nineties.

"And on that note, I better head out before I wake up on your couch tomorrow morning." Ryan threw his head back as he took in the remaining wine that was pooled at the bottom of his glass. Maggie paused the music and transformed her facial expression from merriment to disappointment. She didn't like seeing her two best friends go. Her lips peeled down into a somber line as a twinkle of suspicion lit up her eyes.

As the three of them walked toward the door, Maggie could tell Ryan had a lot on his mind. She asked, "Are you gonna be okay with all of this?"

"Income potential, stale money, taxes going up," he responded, shaking his head side to side, before a wave of realization passed over him. "I can't believe I didn't see this while working in the industry for so many years. And to think that I was pushing this on customers. I'm mad at myself; I'm mad at the financial services industry."

"Well, my life coach has always told me to take my anger and use the energy toward something good," Aaron said as he patted Ryan on the back.

Ryan's eyebrows crumpled together. "You have a life coach?"

"That's beside the point."

"Hold that thought," Maggie turned toward the kitchen and returned with a bottle of water in each hand. She tossed them each one. Just inches before it hit the ground, Ryan bent down and caught his bottle with one hand. "Wow, and for a second I was going to suggest you take an Uber home, but looks like you're still pretty quick on your feet."

"Catching objects has never been a problem, driving after too much wine though isn't worth the risk...I'll be safe and Uber home."

Appendix Five(a):

Income Potential and the Common Rebuttal

This graph should start to summarize the education. The age and income numbers are pulled from Income Percentile by Age Calculator [2020] - DQYDJ[5]

If you start your income at the 50th percentile and grow it over time to the 99th percentile, you have successfully climbed all the tax brackets. I imagine it is a common goal to want to increase one's income over time, either by ambition, industry, or even marriage. However, it doesn't make mathematical sense to defer income into a 401(k), from the lower tax brackets to the higher tax brackets.

Age	50th	75th	90th	99th
25	$31,001	$50,000	$75,500	$164,012
30	$40,210	$64,310	$93,395	$210,000
35	$50,800	$81,800	$131,300	$403,800
40	$50,135	$88,000	$142,600	$363,002
45	$53,002	$90,508	$145,000	$445,500
50	$58,000	$93,520	$140,025	$455,000
55	$54,510	$90,100	$151,500	$495,530
60	$50, 517	$89,200	$155,001	$510,000
65	$55,600	$101,050	$175,445	$565,707

The Common Rebuttal: *I will need less money, and/or I will be in a lower tax bracket at retirement.* To see if that is true for you, find your income and tax rate from your earliest earning years, in the charts

[5] DQYDJ, Calculators and Tools, accessed July 30, 2021, https://dqydj.com/calculators/

below. Then find your current earnings, and your goal for future earnings, perhaps closer to age sixty.

From there, locate your respective tax rate in the chart below. Now, take whatever percentage of that future income goal you see fit for a retirement lifestyle, and find the tax rate associated with that adjusted level of income.

2021 Federal Income Tax Brackets and Rates for Single Filers, Married Couples Filing Jointly, and Heads of Households			
Rate	For Single Individuals	For Married Individuals Filing Joint Returns	For Heads of Households
10%	Up to $9,950	Up to $19,000	Up to $14,200
12%	$9,951 to $40,525	$19,001 to $81,050	$14,201 to $54,200
22%	$40,526 to $86,375	$81,051 to $172,750	$54,201 to $86,350
24%	$86,376 to $164,925	$172,751 to $329,850	$86,351 to $164,900
32%	$164,926 to $209,425	$329,851 to $418,850	$164,901 to $209,400
35%	$209,426 to $523,600	$418,851 to $628,300	$209,401 to $523,600
37%	Over $523,600	Over $628,300	Over $523,600
Source: Internal Revenue Service			

Here is an example to illustrate:

Example of Income Potential for Single Filers and/or Head of Households		
Age	Income	Tax Rate
28 (past age)	$40,000 (past income)	12%
40(current age)	$150,000 (current income)	24%
60 (future age)	$300,000 (future income goal)	35%
Retirement	Goal of retiring off 60% of future income goal ($180,000)	32%

Did **the Common Rebuttal** make sense?

As you can see from this chart, retiring off 60 percent of your future income goal, still places you in a higher tax bracket. You would need to have a retirement goal that is significantly less than your peak earning years. Furthermore, this example does not take into consideration the possibility of increased future tax brackets.

Below represents a hypothetical graph of tax brackets working their way toward the historic top average tax rate. These brackets are made up to illustrate the top bracket going back to the historic average of 60 percent and the lowest bracket staying where it is today. I adjusted the middle brackets to coincide.

2021 Federal Income Tax Brackets and Rates for Single Filers, Married Couples Filing Jointly, and Heads of Households				Historic Top Average
Rate	For Single Individuals	For Married Individuals Filing Joint Returns	For Heads of Households	Tax Rate at 60%
10%	Up to $9,950	Up to $19,000	Up to $14,200	10%
12%	$9,951 to $40,525	$19,001 to $81,050	$14,201 to $54,200	15%
22%	$40,526 to $86,375	$81,051 to $172,750	$54,201 to $86,350	20%
24%	$86,376 to $164,925	$172,751 to $329,850	$86,351 to $164,900	30%
32%	$164,926 to $209,425	$329,851 to $418,850	$164,901 to $209,400	40%
35%	$209,426 to $523,600	$418,851 to $628,300	$209,401 to $523,600	50%
37%	Over $523,600	Over $628,300	Over $523,600	60%
Source: Internal Revenue Service. Tax brackets available on IRS.gov				

Top Federal Tax Rates

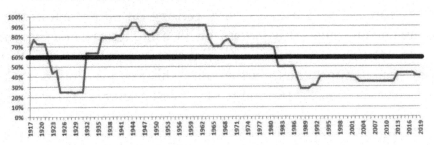

*Black line indicates historic average

Appendix Five(b)

Stale Money

This chart represents a concept I like to call ***Stale Money***. When you stop contributing to your pile, your money grows stale and you put a pause on dollar-cost averaging (an investment strategy that aims to reduce the impact of volatility on large purchases of financial assets such as equities), which is critical for growing market-based assets.

In this example, the first pile of money, $100,000, grows by 12 percent for five straight years to a balance of $176,000 (rounded). The second pile of money, $100,000, grows by 12 percent for three years, then loses 12 percent in the 4th year.

First Pile of Money	
Starting Balance	$100,000.00
YR 1 @ 12%	$112,000.00
YR 2 @ 12%	$125,440.00
YR 3 @ 12%	$140,492.80
YR 4 @ 12%	$157,351.94
YR 5 @ 12%	$176,234.17
Ending Balance	$176,234.17

Second Pile of Money	
Starting Balance	$100,000.00
YR 1 @ 12%	$112,000.00
YR 2 @ 12%	$125,440.00
YR 3 @ 12%	$140,492.80
YR 4 @ -12%	$123,663.66
YR 5 @ ?	
Ending Balance	176,234.17

Here is the question, what **interest rate** would you have to earn in the fifth year to get **back on track** for $176,000? When I ask this question to an audience, the response is often 24 percent. As you can see, from the third pile of money, 24 percent comes up short. You will actually need 43 percent to get back on track, as shown in the fourth pile of money.

Third Pile of Money	
Starting Balance	$100,000.00
YR 1 @ 12%	$112,000.00
YR 2 @ 12%	$125,440.00
YR 3 @ 12%	$140,492.80
YR 4 @ -12%	$123,663.66
YR 5 @ 24%	*$153,305.74*
Target Balance	$176,234.17

Fourth Pile of Money	
Starting Balance	$100,000.00
YR 1 @ 12%	$112,000.00
YR 2 @ 12%	$125,440.00
YR 3 @ 12%	$140,492.80
YR 4 @ -12%	$123,663.66
YR 5 @ 43%	$176,796.14
Target Balance	176,234.17

When your account receives the negative (-12 percent) return you are supposed to contribute money and *dollar-cost average*. If the account is **Stale Money**, and you are not contributing, it is very difficult to get back on pace.

Do you think getting 12 percent returns for five straight years is easy to do? What do you think is an acceptable return for five straight years? Do you think getting a negative (-12) for just one year is a likely possibility? What is the worst one year negative you can recall?

Who gets paid on **Stale Money?**
Do you owe taxes on **Stale Money?**

Chapter Six

Sixth Inning

As if on autopilot, Ryan made his way to The IP Group offices without having to conjure up the directions in his mind. This had been the third time in less than three weeks that he'd driven to the pristine financial campus. If he did end up scoring the job, he'd be able to do the drive in his sleep. His feelings had shifted from the last two visits, and now, as he pulled into the parking lot, he was filled with excitement as opposed to nerves and naivete. Since his first interview, he had noticed his anger rising, like a fire building within him. Every question he had researched at Mike's request had led him to shed more of the shell of his past life as a 401(k) enrollment specialist. As a result, it had expanded the regret within him. Memories of him urging the employees to *max out* flashed in and out of his mind like splices of a movie. He couldn't believe how many times he had told a client they wouldn't need as much money in retirement. He resented that he showed average rates of return and flat compound interest rates. How could he have overlooked so much?

Averages are not how money works; the market does not go up every single year. He kept asking himself why he never questioned this before either. Now, armed with the fact that he had debunked a lot of these myths thanks to Mike and Maggie, he was well aware most people would be at poverty level if they took income potential, rising taxes, and the future cost of living into consideration, among other things.

"Hello, Mr. Anderson." The new receptionist was poised at the front desk, appearing much more confident than she had been the last time he was here.

"Hello–"

"Lucy," she reminded him.

"Lucy. It's great to see you again. Looks like you're a pro now."

"I've still got a few things to learn, but I'm in it to win it." A smile tugged at her lips, emitting a victorious expression. He noticed a book resting on the desk next to her iPad. *Confessions of a CPA.*

"Oh, I see you're brushing up on your reading?"

"Yeah, I've always been a fan of Mr. James' concept and I'm trying to learn everything I can about the industry. He recommended this book as a great place to start." Lucy pushed a strand of hair behind her ear and passed Ryan a professional and confident smile. He thought about how young Lucy looked. She had to be in her early twenties, which made Ryan think about where he was when he started in the industry. If he had met Mike all those years ago who knows where he would be right now.

"Good for you. It looks like he hired the right person for the job." From what Ryan had witnessed, everyone in the building seemed to have the same go-getter personality. The faces he had passed in the hallways and parking lot had smiled with confidence and glowed with passion. Maybe it was something in the water here, but whatever it was, he could attest to wanting to drink from the same fountain.

"I'll let Mr. James know you're here." Lucy punched in a few keys on an iPhone that was sitting face up on the desk. After less than five seconds, the phone danced on the white surface and Lucy smiled. "Do you remember where his office is, Mr. Anderson?"

"I do." Ryan wasn't certain about how to get to Mike's office, but if he got slightly lost it would give him a chance to check out the rest of the area. Maybe he could get a glimpse of some client/advisor interaction.

"Sorry, normally Clara would be here to guide you up, but it sounds like you've met with Mr. James a couple of times already?" Lucy squinted her eyes and Ryan was bolstered with excitement over the fact that maybe he was already a shoe-in. He thought about the other candidates that had been sitting in the waiting area his first day here and wondered if they had even been offered a second interview.

"No worries, Lucy." Ryan turned on a heel and made his way down the sleek hallway toward the elevator. He pressed the black button with a gold number eighteen on it. As he was hoisted to the top floor of the building his stomach did one hefty somersault. A dinging sound alerted him that he reached his destination and the doors parted, catapulting him into a world he was certain he wanted to be a part of. He flanked left off the elevator, unsure of which direction he was headed in. As he passed by the familiar artwork, his eyes scanned the hallways looking for any type of activity. In just a few strides he noticed a pregnant woman and a man sitting in an office, their attention focused on the employee across from them. The employee had his computer screen turned toward them and as he spoke, their eyes grew in response to what they were learning, as if they were opening up to a new concept. Ryan guessed they were consuming the same information that he had recently learned. This young couple was starting their lives out on the right track, avoiding the trap of the IRS and getting ahead on retirement. If only he and his friends had done the same when they had first started their professional jobs. He turned and started to head in the opposite direction, when he nearly bumped into two women. Both of them let out confident giggles as they parted and made a path for him to walk through.

"I'm so sorry, I–"

"You don't know where you're going?" The woman with cropped blonde hair raised an eyebrow in his direction as a wave of heat ascended up his body.

Ryan's quick-witted nature kicked in. "I'm here for my third interview so I thought I'd just make myself at home in an office to speed things up." Ryan flashed a smile.

The woman let out a laugh. "That's one way to do it. Don't worry, I hear good things about you. It's Ryan, right? Here to see Michael James?"

"Yes, that's correct." Ryan extended a hand.

"I'm Dawn, this is Jackie. Nice to meet you." They both shook his hand.

"Go straight down the hall, veer left at conference room 18a and you can't miss his office. It's open…it's always open."

"Thanks."

"I'd wish you luck, but I don't think you need it," Dawn said as Jackie tossed a wink in Ryan's direction. It was like everyone in this building was in on a little secret, and he wanted to be a part of that secret.

As Ryan passed the artwork and the conference room, he wondered how the women knew who he was and what they had heard. Had Mike mentioned him to them? All this time Ryan had thought he was the only one absorbing such impactful information from Mike, but maybe there was a surge of new employees getting hired, all with the same mindset of shedding light on painful taxes and the misinformation that has been told for years. His father's voice echoed in his mind. *The world is full of sheep, Ryan, be a shepherd.* Ryan thought for a second. His dad forgot to mention that sheep get slaughtered. And it was in that moment that he felt even more compelled to reveal the lies and be a voice for education and accurate information.

Just as Ryan started to veer left toward Mike's office, he was caught off guard by a familiar face. While he couldn't quite pinpoint where he knew him from, the man had the same pause of recognition.

"Anderson!" The man took a broad step forward and extended a hand, offering a friendly smile. Obviously struck by Ryan's confusion, he continued. "Bill…Bill McCue from Bail Out Bank." And just like that, the face clicked into place and Ryan was back in the Bail Out Bank office, cubicles away from the man standing in front of him. He and Bill had worked together briefly as 401(k) enrollment specialists, cold calling customers day in and day out in an attempt to build up their portfolios. Having encountered so many different customers, colleagues, and baseball cronies over the years, it was natural that Ryan mixed up faces. And to see someone here, in *his* new territory, it was confusing to say the least, like the blending of two very separate worlds.

"Bill! I'm so sorry, I recognized you, but I couldn't place you for a second. How are you?"

A genuine and relaxed smile passed across Bill's lips. He looked younger and more in shape than Ryan had remembered. "Great!

Now that I'm here." He paused, assessing Ryan from head to toe. "Are you here for an interview?"

"I am." Ryan noticed Bill wasn't wearing a suit and instead of carrying a briefcase or bag, he simply held a phone in his hand.

"Well, I'm really happy to hear that, bud. I gotta tell you…I've been with these guys for a couple of years now and I've never been happier. He took one step closer to Ryan as if he was starting a classified conversation. "These guys are doing a good thing. They are ripping away all of the things we used to push at Bail Out Bank, and they are spreading the truth the way it should be spread." Bill shrugged his shoulders and transformed his lips into a matter-of-fact smile. "Saving lives if you ask me."

Hearing this from an old colleague eased any doubts that Ryan still had, which were minimal. "Sounds like it. I gotta be honest, Bill…I don't know how I missed so much all these years."

Bill laughed. "Ryan, wait till you get into the training. There is so much that advisors don't know, let alone the clients. I look back at it and I can't believe what we were taught at the bank. Monetize your relationships, turn everyone into a fee generator, charge everyone one to 2 percent. And it was all garbage."

"How's the training here?" Ryan asked. "Please tell me it's better than what we experienced at the bank."

"Make more dials!" They both laughed and blurted out the same line as if on cue.

Ryan recalled his training at Bail Out Bank. It was labeled, *Growing Your Book of Business*," which essentially meant, *Look How Much Money You Can Make Charging Fees*. And this was always paired with a manager hollering at them to *make more dials*.

As their laughter came to an end, Bill asked, "Are you meeting with Mike?"

"Yes, right around the corner, right?"

"The one with the open door, you can't miss him. I won't keep you, bud, but gosh it's good to see someone coming over from the other side. You'd be surprised at how many advisors have recently come over." Bill used one hand to offer a shake and another to grip Ryan's shoulder in a friendly gesture. "Hey and let me know if you need a reference. You were always one of the good guys." He tossed a fist bump in his direction.

Ryan gave one hard knock on the doorframe of Mike's office. With Mike's eyes still focused on his computer screen, he said, "It's open." Then he rose to his feet and reached across the top of his desk extending a hand. "I'm glad you came back, Ryan. Take a seat."

As Ryan dropped into the chair, he suddenly felt like he was home. This was where he was meant to be; this was what he was supposed to be doing with his life. "Well, to be honest, Mike, I couldn't *not* come back."

"Really? That's a bold statement." Mike leaned back in his chair and planted his gaze on Ryan.

"This whole thing…what the government is doing to hard-working people, what the financial services industry is doing, is bad. It's real bad, Mike."

"You're absolutely right, Ryan. Do you want to know why?" Mike projected his computer screen onto the large TV on the wall. After a few clicks on his mouse, an elaborate spreadsheet was thrown onto the screen, a collage of stripes and numbers. "Take this scenario I've been working on as an example." He clicked again, displaying another sheet as he summarized the sums of money on the wall. "Let's say you are maxing out your 401(k) for thirty straight years at an 8 percent return. We both know the market doesn't do that, but let's just say that it did. You would have approximately $2,220,000 inside your 401(k). Now, let's say Wall Street, the mutual funds, and the 401(k) plan administrators, take approximately 1 percent in total costs. When we redo the math, your new balance is $1,850,000. That 1 percent charge generates $370,000 for the proverbial Wall Street. That is why they hire somebody like you to go tell as many people as they can to max out their 401(k). And that's just the first thirty years on the way to retirement. Keep in mind that it gets worse from retirement to mortality." Mike pulled up another sheet that showed the fees and costs generated from a hypothetical person aged sixty to eighty-eight. Associated with that was a 1 percent charge equaling another $260,000. The total amount taken from the 401(k) and qualified plan participant resulted in $630,000.

As Ryan absorbed the information, he thought about his largest account. Shexxon Oil had over one thousand employees enrolled in their 401(k) plan. Ryan stared at the spreadsheets that Mike was putting together and he immediately knew this spreadsheet was coming together as part of a massive education strategy. He knew the purpose of the strategy was to get this information communicated to people of all ages. While it was always right there in front of everybody, the entire time, nobody had actually done the math.

Ryan thought for a second, marinating in anger. They had always talked about 1 percent in fees, but the total amount of fees from 401(k)s, mutual funds and administrative costs could total well over 2 or 3 percent.

Mike's voice sliced through his thoughts, bringing him back to the discussion. "We also need to take into consideration that these balances haven't even been taxed yet. This is what we've been talking about this whole time."

"Not yet, but they certainly will be." Ryan's reply came fast, followed by another bout of anger.

"That's right! You're paying fees and costs, expense ratios, administrative charges, on a larger balance." Mike's next sentence stretched out slowly and deliberately. "You're even paying the fees and costs on the money that ultimately will go to the IRS, so technically you're paying the IRS's fees."

"That's right. The fees, administrative costs, and the expense ratios, are on the entire balance, but the entire balance doesn't belong to you. A little less than half of that balance goes to the IRS. So, with that said, we are paying the fees and costs on the IRS's money." He sat with eyes wide, stunned by his own words.

"Unfortunately, the math is right, Ryan. In many cases, individuals max out their 401(k)s, ride the market up and down repeatedly, and after paying Wall Street 1 or 2 percent in fees, the participant lines up to pay the IRS nearly half. I've been studying this for a while, and net of the fees and costs, and net of the taxes, Americans are struggling to just get their money back." Mike leaned back in his chair. "Do you remember when I asked you what tax bracket you'll fall under in the future?"

Ryan nodded.

"And do you think taxes are going up or down in the future?"

"Well, with the deficit, COVID relief packages, stimulus bills, and costs of social programs, taxes have to go up, right?"

Mike replied, "I don't have a crystal ball, but I can tell you that you're not the only one that feels that way. And if the tax rates go up, the real value of your 401(k) would go down."

Ryan wiped a hand down his face and shook his head. "We have to get this out there, we have to help people."

"That leads to my next question." He sat back and for the first time Ryan could see fatigue. Mike had the look of a seasoned officer. He noticed some gray hair creeping along the sides of his head, likely resulting from the amount of time he spent building this company. Mike's eyes narrowed and he stared directly at Ryan. "Do you want to join this fight?" Before Ryan could respond, Mike continued, passionately pushing several questions out. "Do you want to tell people the truth? Do you want to educate and help people understand what no one in finance wants to tell them?" Stunned, Ryan didn't have a chance to answer before Mike continued, his voice solid, his determination unwavering. With confidence and conviction echoing throughout the room, he said, "You have to be part of the solution, or you are part of the problem. Advisors and clients need to know what is happening out there, people are not fees, their life savings are not just part of your assets under management, people are not just tax revenue. They deserve the truth. This entire organization is built on education, math, and the truth. We *need* guys like you to help us get the job done."

Ryan had never felt so clear and inspired about the path he wanted to take. While he had said yes to joining the fight, Mike insisted he think about the decision, wanting him absolutely committed. For the next twenty minutes, Mike reminded him of the difficulty involved in being in the financial services industry. "Most people would rather keep their head in the sand than know the truth," he had said. "Come back and see me when you have a solid grip on your answer. I'll give you a few days to think about it." Mike abruptly stood up and extended his hand once again, offering a firm grip as if he was sealing a deal.

***

As Ryan pushed his way out The IP Group doors once again, his mind was swirling with thoughts. He was pretty sure that he was just offered what could be his dream job, but he knew that if he accepted, he had to go all in, he had to shift his thinking from something he had been exercising for twelve years to an unorthodox approach to financial planning. And he knew he would receive some backlash for it, but he didn't care. He could hear his longtime colleagues as they questioned him about his paradigm shift, but once he explained the math, they would understand. They needed this information and Ryan would do everything in his power to get it to them.

On his route back to his current office the highway billboards caused him to think even deeper about the 401(k) situation. A massive sign showcasing an older couple enjoying themselves on an alluring island, complete with shimmering green-blue water in the background, caught his eye. They were both enjoying a frozen drink, smiling at one another, their bright white teeth vibrant against glowing tan skin. They painted the picture of a successfully retired couple well into their seventies, but Ryan knew that a more accurate portrait should actually portray a couple with worrisome expressions, struggling to pay a mortgage that they likely refinanced in their later years.

If the billboard was painting an accurate picture, Ryan was certain it should include dollar signs and question marks inside thought bubbles over their heads. And that's when it hit him. Something he and Maggie had missed was provisional income. Known as the income level that determines how your Social Security income can be taxed, provisional income could make or break a person in their retirement years.

Nearly missing the exit that led to his office, Ryan jerked the steering wheel right and made it by just a couple of inches. The tail of his Mercedes swerved slightly to the left, causing his stomach to leap into a series of flip flops. His palms, slick with sweat, gripped the steering wheel as he guided himself slowly and calmly to his office. The secrets he was uncovering about taxes and 401(k)s would kill him if he didn't do something about it.

Appendix Six

Accumulation Phase and Distribution Phase

Using the same graph from appendix three, I adjusted the return sequence to reflect two bad years out of thirty-five total years. At age forty and age fifty, I entered a negative (-35 percent) return. The new balance, net of fees, but gross of taxes, is $1,245,164.

In the *Accumulation Phase* you have contributed $705,600. By turning $705,600 into $1,245,164, you have earned $539,564 of growth and the 401(k) provider in this example has earned 45 percent of your total growth. The 401(k) provider has pocketed $244,635, nearly half of your gross earnings. Remember, you still owe taxes on the entire balance in the *Distribution Phase.*

Accumulation Phase

Age	Contribution	Growth Rate	Gross Balance	Annual "Fees"1.25%	Net Balance
30	$ 19,600.00	7%	$ 20,972.00	$ 262.15	$ 20,709.85
31	$ 19,600.00	7%	$ 43,412.04	$ 542.65	$ 42,588.89
32	$ 19,600.00	7%	$ 67,422.88	$ 842.79	$ 65,699.33
33	$ 19,600.00	7%	$ 93,114.48	$ 1,163.93	$ 90,106.35
34	$ 19,600.00	7%	$ 120,604.50	$ 1,507.56	$ 115,878.23
35	$ 19,600.00	7%	$ 150,018.81	$ 1,875.24	$ 143,086.48
36	$ 19,600.00	7%	$ 181,492.13	$ 2,268.65	$ 171,805.88
37	$ 19,600.00	7%	$ 215,168.58	$ 2,689.61	$ 202,114.68
38	$ 19,600.00	7%	$ 251,202.38	$ 3,140.03	$ 234,094.68
39	$ 19,600.00	7%	$ 289,758.55	$ 3,621.98	$ 267,831.33
40	$ 19,600.00	NEGATIVE (-35%)	$ 188,343.06	$ 2,354.29	$ 184,476.07

Balls and Strikes:

41	$ 19,600.00	7%	$ 222,499.07	$ 2,781.24	$ 215,580.16
42	$ 19,600.00	7%	$ 259,046.00	$ 3,238.08	$ 248,404.70
43	$ 19,600.00	7%	$ 298,151.22	$ 3,726.89	$ 283,038.14
44	$ 19,600.00	7%	$ 339,993.81	$ 4,249.92	$ 319,572.88
45	$ 19,600.00	7%	$ 384,765.38	$ 4,809.57	$ 358,105.42
46	$ 19,600.00	7%	$ 432,670.95	$ 5,408.39	$ 398,736.41
47	$ 19,600.00	7%	$ 483,929.92	$ 6,049.12	$ 441,570.83
48	$ 19,600.00	7%	$ 538,777.01	$ 6,734.71	$ 486,718.08
49	$ 19,600.00	7%	$ 597,463.41	$ 7,468.29	$ 534,292.05
50	$ 19,600.00	NEGATIVE (-35%)	$ 388,351.21	$ 4,854.39	$ 355,175.44
51	$ 19,600.00	7%	$ 436,507.80	$ 5,456.35	$ 395,553.38
52	$ 19,600.00	7%	$ 488,035.34	$ 6,100.44	$ 438,113.67
53	$ 19,600.00	7%	$ 543,169.82	$ 6,789.62	$ 482,964.01
54	$ 19,600.00	7%	$ 602,163.71	$ 7,527.05	$ 530,216.44
55	$ 19,600.00	7%	$ 665,287.16	$ 8,316.09	$ 579,987.50
56	$ 19,600.00	7%	$ 732,829.27	$ 9,160.37	$ 632,398.26
57	$ 19,600.00	7%	$ 805,099.32	$ 10,063.74	$ 687,574.40
58	$ 19,600.00	7%	$ 882,428.27	$ 11,030.35	$ 745,646.25
59	$ 19,600.00	7%	$ 965,170.25	$ 12,064.63	$ 806,748.86
60	$ 19,600.00	7%	$ 1,053,704.16	$ 13,171.30	$ 871,021.98
61	$ 19,600.00	7%	$ 1,148,435.45	$ 14,355.44	$ 938,610.08
62	$ 19,600.00	7%	$ 1,249,797.94	$ 15,622.47	$ 1,009,662.31
63	$ 19,600.00	7%	$ 1,358,255.79	$ 16,978.20	$ 1,084,332.47
64	$ 19,600.00	7%	$ 1,474,305.70	$ 18,428.82	$ 1,162,778.92
65	$ 19,600.00	7%	$ 1,598,479.10	$ 19,980.99	$ 1,245,164.46
	$705,600.00			$244,635.33	

In the ***Distribution Phase***, I take the balance, net of fees and volatility, and apply the *safe withdrawal rate*. Remember, the safe withdrawal rate is what you could safely withdraw annually during retirement and run the balance down to zero by the approximate mortality age. This is NOT to be confused with interest income which assumes the balance stays intact.

Now repeat the "fees" and apply taxes. The fees erode another $121,913 and you get to spend $876,595, net 20 percent of our hypothetical taxes.

Distribution Phase

Age	Account Balance	SWR @ 4%	Gross Withdrawal	Net Withdrawal Taxes at 20%	"Fees" @ 1.25%
66	*$1,245,164.46	4%	$ 49,806.58	$ 39,845.26	$ 15,564.56
67	*$1,095,744.72	4%	$ 49,806.58	$ 39,845.26	$ 13,696.81
68	*$964,255.36	4%	$ 49,806.58	$ 39,845.26	$ 12,053.19
69	*$848,544.71	4%	$ 49,806.58	$ 39,845.26	$ 10,606.81
70	*$746,719.35	4%	$ 49,806.58	$ 39,845.26	$ 9,333.99
71	*$657,113.03	4%	$ 49,806.58	$ 39,845.26	$ 8,213.91
72	*$578,259.46	4%	$ 49,806.58	$ 39,845.26	$ 7,228.24
73	*$508,868.33	4%	$ 49,806.58	$ 39,845.26	$ 6,360.85
74	*$447,804.13	4%	$ 49,806.58	$ 39,845.26	$ 5,597.55
75	*$394,067.63	4%	$ 49,806.58	$ 39,845.26	$ 4,925.85
76	*$346,779.52	4%	$ 49,806.58	$ 39,845.26	$ 4,334.74
77	*$305,165.97	4%	$ 49,806.58	$ 39,845.26	$ 3,814.57
78	*$268,546.06	4%	$ 49,806.58	$ 39,845.26	$ 3,356.83
79	*$236,320.53	4%	$ 49,806.58	$ 39,845.26	$ 2,954.01
80	*$207,962.07	4%	$ 49,806.58	$ 39,845.26	$ 2,599.53
81	*$183,006.62	4%	$ 49,806.58	$ 39,845.26	$ 2,287.58

82	*$161,045.82	4%	$ 49,806.58	$ 39,845.26	$ 2,013.07
83	*$141,720.33	4%	$ 49,806.58	$ 39,845.26	$ 1,771.50
84	*$124,713.89	4%	$ 49,806.58	$ 39,845.26	$ 1,558.92
85	*$109,748.22	4%	$ 49,806.58	$ 39,845.26	$ 1,371.85
86	*$96,578.43	4%	$ 49,806.58	$ 39,845.26	$ 1,207.23
87	*$84,989.02	4%	$ 49,806.58	$ 39,845.26	$ 1,062.36
				$876,595.78	$121,913.97

*Safe Withdrawal Rate (SWR)

Take a moment and study this graph. I don't care what tax brackets, contribution, withdrawal rate, or interest rate you use, just start doing your math. If the projections you are using only show *flat returns*, the same number repeated every single year, stop using them. You should enter a negative return into your projection from time to time. If anyone tells you to "max out" your 401(k) without discussing your future *Tax Liability* and/or your **income potential** take a moment to question their motives and your goals.

Now, look at your total employee contributions of $705,600. You have made a 1.39 percent real *spendable* rate of return. You put in $705,600 over thirty-five years and got to spend, net of fees, volatility, and taxes, $876,505. Wall Street collected $366,549 which is a lot more than you did.

Total "Fees" Accumulation and Distribution	$ 366,549.30
Total Employee Contributions	$ 705,600.00
Total After-Tax Spendable Dollars	$ 876,595.78
Real Spendable Rate of Return	**1.39%**

In this example, you will notice that the balance on the account is dropping by more than the gross withdrawal. At the beginning it drops by a lot more than the withdrawal and toward the end it drops a lot less than the withdrawal. According to the safe withdrawal rate, if you withdraw a *safe*, consistent amount annually, (in this example we used 4 percent), the remaining balance, if still invested conservatively, will fluctuate. The remaining balance in some years may earn a conservative 3 percent and, in some years may lose a conservative -3 percent. These fluctuations, along with your consistent withdrawals, will ultimately cause the remaining balance to reach $0 or very near $0 at about the average mortality age. It is difficult to predict the timeline and amounts of these positive and negative returns. However, through simulation, it is safe to predict that the balance should ultimately work its way down to a very low number, if not zero. So, in this example, I simply took the starting balance and reduced it annually toward a very low number at about the average mortality age. Again, please feel free to make your own assumptions but the safe withdrawal rate is widely accepted. The point of this chart is to give an example of how fees and taxes could also erode your balance during your distribution years.

The idea is that the SWR is a percentage of the starting balance that can be consistently withdrawn and not cause the individual to run out of money before death. If you withdraw more than the SWR you could run out of money before you die. If you withdraw less than the SWR, you could be living below your means. It is also very important to understand that the safe withdrawal rate can fluctuate based on the interest rate environment and stock market conditions. While, at times it has also been referred to as the "4 percent rule," suggesting that 4 percent is the safe withdrawal rate, current studies are suggesting that the safe withdrawal rate is closer to 3 percent or even 2 percent. [6]If we dropped the SWR down to 2 percent in the chart above, doing so would drastically reduce your spendable dollars, it would not, however, change the amount you paid in fees or negate your tax liability.

[6] Christine Benz, "Retirees: Are You Spending Too Much?", Morningstar, January 2021, accessed August 2, 2021, https://www.morningstar.com/articles/844210/retirees-are-you-spending-too-much?utm_medium=referral&utm_campaign=linkshare&utm_source=link

Chapter Seven

Seventh Inning

Ryan's workday was injected with thoughts about provisional income. Now, after what seemed like the longest day ever, he sipped a craft beer at his kitchen table, his laptop and a notebook spread out before him, ready to take part in a deeper investigation. He had attempted to go to sleep two hours ago but thoughts about his friends and family losing part of their Social Security benefits were racing through his mind.

Provisional income was defined by the IRS as the sum of wages, taxable and nontaxable interest, taxable interest, dividends, pensions, self-employment and other taxable income plus half, or 50 percent of your annual Social Security benefits. Ryan scoured websites ranging from IRS.gov to AARP.org to summarize as much as he could about provisional income. So many people were relying on their Social Security, and so few knew the truth.

"So, basically if I show too much money on my tax returns during retirement, up to 85 percent of my Social Security can be taxed at ordinary income tax rates," he said out loud to himself as he squeezed his forehead. He thought for a second and then spoke out loud again. "Wait a minute, Social Security contributions are made after taxes. Don't we pay for our Social Security benefits with after-tax dollars?" Ryan furiously banged away at his keyboard Googling these questions. In only a few minutes, he discovered that he was right, and summed it all up to himself. "So, I make after-tax contributions paying for Social Security and then in retirement if I withdraw too much taxable income from my 401(k), I will pay taxes for the second time on my Social Security benefits, because up to 85 percent of my Social Security can be taxed as ordinary income for the second time around."

With a little more effort, Ryan became a dedicated student of provisional income and its impact on Social Security. He quickly learned that depending on filing status, it took as little as $25,000 of reportable provisional income to trigger a double tax on your Social Security. It took as little as $34,000 of reportable provisional income to trigger as much as 85 percent of your Social Security taxed as ordinary income tax rates.

Taking it a step further, he discovered that provisional income played a role in determining the premiums that are paid on Medicare insurance during retirement. Using both of his index fingers to massage his temples, he repeated what he'd learned to himself. "So, if I am fortunate enough to do well in my retirement accounts, it will trigger additional taxes due on my Social Security and Medicare premiums. On the other hand, if I don't do well in my retirement accounts then I get these benefits free of additional taxes."

Maybe as a CPA, Maggie knew something that he didn't.

***

As soon as he pressed stop on his phone alarm clock, he shot up in bed and called Maggie, spilling everything he had learned, expressing both excitement and disbelief. He had hoped that as a CPA, maybe she knew something that he didn't.

"Oh my gosh." Ryan could hear her criticizing herself with a long list of swear words in the background before she came back. "I knew all of this, but I somehow forgot," Maggie responded, breathing heavily as she pounded her feet on the treadmill. "Social Security benefits can be taxed at all levels, federal tax, as well as state and local taxes. And yes, I am, you are, we are all making contributions to Social Security post tax."

"Which means that if you owe taxes on Social Security in retirement, it will be the second time that you would pay taxes on the same dollar, right?" Ryan asked.

The two of them dove deeper into the conversation, noting that the Social Security program was in dire straits and if it remained like this, there wouldn't be enough money to continue it. And in turn, the only solution would be to increase taxes to fund the program.

"I think that's called double taxation. This could lead to bad things in the future," Maggie said. "It will likely mean more after-tax contributions to the Social Security program and getting less dollars during retirement from the program."

"It could also mean lowering the provisional income limits that trigger the taxes owed on Social Security or making Social Security 100 percent taxable during retirement," Ryan added, spinning the conversation out of control.

The two of them came to the conclusion that if Social Security was even available to them when they retired, it would likely be the result of them being taxed more.

"Surely, there has to be a way to avoid these pitfalls," Ryan declared.

Appendix Seven

Provisional Income and Social Security

This is a picture of a John Doe paystub. You are making Social Security contributions with after-tax dollars. This means you have already paid taxes on the money you are contributing to Social Security.

In the W-2 Wage and Tax Statement example below, box 3 and box 5 represent the total wages earned, or $52,191. Think of this as gross income. From this number, subtract box 12a which represents a pre-tax contribution into a 401(k) of $5,000. This net number, represented in box 1, $47,191, is the amount of income you will owe taxes on. The amount of federal income tax withheld is shown on the paystub in box 2, resulting in a total of $3,946. After the pre-tax contribution to the 401(k) and the required federal taxes are withheld, then a mandatory, after-tax, Social Security tax withholding, box 4, will be deducted from your pay.

a Employee's social security number				
555 55 5555	OMB No. 1545-0008	This information is being furnished to the Internal Revenue Service. If you are required to file a tax return, a negligence penalty or other sanction may be imposed on you if this income is taxable and you fail to report it.		

b Employer identification number (EIN) 66-5555555		1 Wages, tips, other compensation 47191.10	2 Federal income tax withheld 3946.82
c Employer's name, address, and ZIP code ABC DEMO CO. 1313 MAIN ST ANYTOWN, IL 60000		3 Social security wages 52191.10	4 Social security tax withheld 3235.85
		5 Medicare wages and tips 52191.10	6 Medicare tax withheld 756.77
		7 Social security tips	8 Allocated tips
d Control number		9 Verification code	10 Dependent care benefits
e Employee's first name and initial Last name Suff. JOHN M DOE 2626 OAK ST ANYTOWN, IL 60000		11 Nonqualified plans	12a See instructions for box 12 D 5000.00
		13 Statutory employee ☐ Retirement plan ☒ Third-party sick pay ☐	12b AA 2500.00
		14 Other	12c DD 13580.66
			12d
f Employee's address and ZIP code			

15 State IL	Employer's state ID number 333661111	16 State wages, tips, etc. 47191.10	17 State income tax 1075.11	18 Local wages, tips, etc.	19 Local income tax	20 Locality name

Form **W-2** Wage and Tax Statement

2017

Copy C—For EMPLOYEE'S RECORDS (See *Notice to Employee on the back of Copy B.*)

Department of the Treasury—Internal Revenue Service

Safe, accurate, FAST! Use **e-file**

Balls and Strikes:

This is a picture of a John Doe tax return that shows where your Social Security benefits are added to your provisional income to be taxed for the second time. If you report too much income from tax qualified accounts, like your 401(k) and/or IRA, you could be "double taxed" on your Social Security.

1	Wages, salaries, tips, etc. Attach Form(s) W-2				1	
2a	Tax-exempt interest	2a		b Taxable interest	2b	
3a	Qualified dividends	3a		b Ordinary dividends	3b	
4a	IRA distributions	4a		b Taxable amount	4b	
5a	Pensions and annuities	5a		b Taxable amount	5b	
6a	Social security benefits	6a		b Taxable amount	6b	
7	Capital gain or (loss). Attach Schedule D if required. If not required, check here ▶ ☐				7	
8	Other income from Schedule 1, line 10				8	
9	Add lines 1, 2b, 3b, 4b, 5b, 6b, 7, and 8. This is your **total income** ▶				9	
10	Adjustments to income from Schedule 1, line 26				10	
11	Subtract line 10 from line 9. This is your **adjusted gross income** ▶				11	
12a	Standard deduction or itemized deductions (from Schedule A)	12a				
b	Charitable contributions if you take the standard deduction (see instructions)	12b				
c	Add lines 12a and 12b				12c	
13	Qualified business income deduction from Form 8995 or Form 8995-A				13	
14	Add lines 12c and 13				14	
15	**Taxable income.** Subtract line 14 from line 11. If zero or less, enter -0-				15	

Chapter Eight

Eighth Inning

After he got off the phone with Maggie, Ryan was prepping himself to call Mike. His eyes felt like sandpaper beneath his lids from last night's lack of sleep. Not normally one to pull an all-nighter, he was up until two in the morning going over the math. Ryan concluded that provisional income affects everyone, all backgrounds, all careers. However, he also discovered it was largely the middle-class families that relied solely on their employer sponsored 401(k)s and subsequent rollover IRA's that could be impacted the most. Ryan found some statistics that suggested the median retirement income for a sixty-five-year-old was roughly $40,000-45,000 annually. [7]He wondered if it was a coincidence that the number was over the top threshold of provisional income triggering the most amount of taxes due on Social Security. Ryan discovered that most Americans have just enough inside their 401(k)s to obligate maximum taxes due on their Social Security. Unfortunately, these people were simply told that this was the right way.

He was so eager to talk to Mike, but he promised himself he would wait until seven to make the call. In one of their exchanges, Mike had mentioned that he goes to the gym at five-thirty every morning and gets to the office by seven, so Ryan knew it would be safe to contact him by then. His head hazy, he went about getting ready for the day, all the while thinking about how he was going to give his two-week notice to his boss. Would he tell him everything he learned? Would his former boss be able to walk away from all the fees he generates from his clients? Would he let him in on the secret and attempt to pull him over to the other side? Or would he quietly walk away, stating that he had received a better offer? The thing he

---

[7] Pension Right Center, April 16, 2021, accessed August 3, 2021, https://www.pensionrights.org/publications/statistic/income-today%E2%80%99s-older-adults

knew for certain was that all of his past colleagues and bosses would one day know that there would be a much different way to save for the future. A way that was less reliant on the 401(k) and didn't involve losing massive sums to taxes.

After half a ring, Michael James picked up the phone. It was obvious to Ryan that the man was fired up on his post-gym energy. "Ryan, how are you?" His words came through the phone fueled by adrenaline.

"I'm good, Mike, sorry for the early call."

"Oh no worries, I was just taking souls at the gym."

Ryan laughed, picking up on the David Goggins' reference. "I was actually hoping we could get together. Any chance you're free to meet up soon?"

***

On his way to the IP office, Maggie called him to wish him good luck. As always, he had kept her updated on his exchanges with Mike, who had suggested Ryan come in for a think tank session and to discuss provisional income further with a few other employees.

"Ryan, this could change the financial services industry as we know it," she said over the phone in between bites of her sandwich. "You realize that right?"

"I have no doubt about that," Ryan said as he pulled into the IP parking lot. "I'll call ya later." He hung up with Maggie and started walking toward the building. It was nearing lunch time and several employees emerged from the building, some in groups and some on solo missions. A cluster of women paused their conversation as Ryan walked by, each one passing him a friendly smile as if they were welcoming him into their world, inviting him into their web of knowledge.

"Hi, Ryan." One of the girls waved. He knew that he had seen her in the hallway on one of his visits with Mike, but he was unsure of her name.

He extended his undivided attention and locked eyes with her. "How are you today?" He cocked his head as he continued to walk, suddenly drenched in confidence. Something about this place and this group of people made the impossible feel very possible.

After riding the elevator to the eighteenth floor, the receptionist led Ryan to a set of double doors.

"They're right inside," she said.

"Thank you," he replied. He pushed through a set of double doors and was immediately greeted by a security guard.

"They are expecting you, Mr. Anderson," the guard said before he told him to go through another set of double doors that were made of tinted glass. The IP Group emblem was layered over the tint in bold print, the colossal I and P taking up most of the surface. As he pushed through the second set of doors, he found himself in the most amazing conference room he had ever seen. The room was huge but more impressive was how small it felt against the Houston skyline. The opposite outer wall was all glass. He could see expansive downtown Houston, the medical center, and The Galleria all at once. The conference room table looked like it could seat fifty and there was an outdoor terrace equipped with patio furniture and a mounted flatscreen. Two other men were wrapping up a friendly conversation at the table, as Mike emerged from his seat.

"Ryan, thanks for coming in." He shifted gears when he noticed that Ryan was in awe of the space. "Kind of a fun room, huh?" The two of them stood side by side, taking in the view together.

"Absolutely. Do you have meetings up here?" Ryan asked.

With a laugh, Mike replied, "What do you think we're doing right now?"

Slightly embarrassed, Ryan shook his head and smiled. "What an amazing view."

"I know, right, and the answer is yes, we have meetings up here. Clients and advisors use this space quite a bit, and we do a lot of our trainings in here." Mike walked closer to the window.

"I like to think the setup gives them a chance to step away, enjoy the Houston skyline and most certainly get a different perspective on life."

"And on their financial planning," one of the other men chimed in.

Mike nodded. "If we are truly going to set people free, we have to start by creating a vision for them. We can't be just like everybody else." He turned toward the two other men. "I'd like you to meet some of the knuckleheads on our team. This is Patrick, previously at Chase Fargo. We like to call him Wolf." The man stood, walked around the table, and presented Ryan with a confident handshake. "He has twenty years in retirement planning and financial services. He started at the big banks and now he is one of the top advisors here at The IP Group. Wolf has been with me since day one." A proud smile gleamed across both Mike's and Wolf's faces.

Mike turned toward the other man, who looked to be about the same age as Wolf. "This is Josh. Previously from North York Mutual. Josh is from the insurance side and has twenty years amongst all the major mutual insurance companies. This guy has been with us for only a couple of years and has already put a dent in Houston."

Josh stood and offered Ryan a handshake. "Howdy."

"I've always said that the investments and insurances have to work together to build what is right for the client. These two gentlemen have helped me create something explosive. And gentlemen, this firecracker here...is Blue." Mike turned toward Ryan, making a moment out of the introduction.

Without missing a beat, Josh asked, "Why Blue?"

"Well, you may not be able to tell from his polished appearance right now, but Ryan Anderson here is one of the top college baseball umpires in the country." Mike paused. "And I believe I just made the decision to call him Blue, like the umpires of old."

Followed by a mutual laugh between the four of them, Wolf said, "Well, Blue, Mike speaks very highly of you, so we are happy that you're here."

"Let's not waste any more time. Grab a seat and let's have some fun." Mike gestured to the leather chairs. As he lowered himself into a seat he said, "You came back so that must mean something, right?"

"I did and first of all, I'd like to say thank you. This whole experience has been incredible and very eye opening."

"It's my pleasure."

"Meeting you has led me to believe we must change the way people think about their retirement strategies. And we need to educate more people on provisional income." Ryan smoothed a hand on the smooth mahogany tabletop, a piece of furniture that he had seen in countless finance movies over the years.

"The IRS threshold above which Social Security income may be taxable…a topic that is near and dear to my heart," Mike shot back.

"Yes, but look at this." Ryan paused, looking around the room for something to annotate his thoughts on. His eyes landed on a white board. "May I?" He gestured toward the wall.

"He's a white boarder," Josh said, as he let out a laugh. The secret joke causing a smile to ripple between the three men.

"Be my guest." Mike angled his chair so he was facing the board and placed his interlaced hands behind his head.

Ryan rose from his chair, grabbed the marker, and planted himself in front of the white board, front and center on the massive wall. Like a teacher, he went to work writing out several different columns. As high as he could reach, he wrote the words *asset/income source*. A few steps to his right he wrote the words, *provisional income*, and a couple more steps to the right he wrote the words *tax SS*, for Social Security. Ryan then moved back under asset/income source and listed rows that read 401(k) then IRA and beneath that, dividends/interest. At the bottom of the row, he wrote rental property. Ryan was suggesting that these assets or sources of income are common places that people get money from during retirement. To the right, underneath provisional income he wrote *yes* beside 401(k), IRA, dividends/interest, and a final yes beside rental property. His goal was to demonstrate that all these assets counted as provisional income during retirement years. Ryan slid to the right one more time and caught his breath for dramatic effect as he wrote one very large *YES* under the words tax SS. The yes was so large that it covered all the assets and income sources. He turned to face his audience and continued the speech that he had repeated to himself over and over again.

"All of these common sources of retirement income count as provisional income and could trigger taxes owed on your Social

Security. If an individual withdraws too much money from these sources, they will pay taxes for the second time on their Social Security benefits." Showing slight frustration, he continued. "This is unbelievable, these are the most common sources of retirement income and if you do well in these areas you will lose out on your Social Security benefits."

Ryan paused. He could feel his exhaustion kicking in from the sleepless night before. The three men in the room watched as Ryan was coming to the conclusion that they had already experienced. Each one of them joined The IP Group learning that what they've been taught to believe was wrong. The men in the room watched as Ryan grew more frustrated. They had witnessed this so many times before. He turned toward Josh, Wolf and Mike and with an exasperated expression on his face he said, "Why have people been told to max out their 401(k)s?"

After a long minute of silence, Wolf responded. "Ryan, it's because that's what advisors are trained to tell people. Advisors all across America are telling people to max out their 401(k)s because that is what advisors are trained to tell you."

Following up Wolf's words, Mike joined in. "The answer, Ryan, or the *reason*, is money, plain and simple. Most of the revenue or income that financial advisors make comes from assets under management or what they call *fee-based advisory*. Advisors get paid by how much of your money they have in their control. Where does the majority of this money come from?" He pressed on answering his own question. "When the 401(k)s rollover into IRAs." He paused, before he summed up his final answer. "So, advisors tell you to put as much money as you can into your retirement accounts so that when you change jobs or retire, they can park that money under their management, and charge you a fee. It's a system, Ryan. They tell as many people as they can to put as much money into these qualified accounts in the hopes that someday that money will sit underneath them, and they can charge a fee. Their training teaches them to tell clients that they will retire in a lower tax bracket. They are also told to tell the client that they will not need as much money in retirement. Trust me, you would be absolutely shocked and devastated to learn how many fee-based advisors do not understand or care about your provisional income and the taxes you owe on Social Security. We at The IP Group, the ones actually doing the math are considered the oddballs." He looked around the room, taking the time to lock eye contact with each one of them.

Josh chimed in. "Ryan, in some cases the advisor's only employment requirement is to grow their assets under management. So much so, that if they do not grow the size of their book or the amount of new accounts, then they are penalized or even terminated. Think about that for a second. What if you're headed into retirement and want to make withdrawals? If you do, your advisor could land in hot water. Seems a bit odd, doesn't it?"

"Ryan, here is some math that we are happy to show clients," Mike added. "If a fee-based advisor has twenty clients each with $500,000, then that advisor has ten million under management. If the advisor is charging 1 percent in fees, then that advisor could earn approximately $100,000 per year in income. The advisor would not want those balances to go down. If all twenty clients started withdrawing money, year after year, the total amount of money under management would decrease and in doing so the advisor's compensation would also decrease. Believe me when I tell you that some of these advisors are not concerned with your provisional income, your tax liability, or the taxes you could owe on your Social Security. They are only concerned about growing the total amount of assets under management, which is how they get paid."

Ryan leaned in and put his elbows on the table, his palms pressed together in prayer beneath his chin. "So, let me get this straight, the 401(k) plan administrator is charging administrative costs and the mutual funds that are inside the 401(k) have expense ratios, all of which take money out of the client's pocket. Then, if we change jobs or if we retire, people are likely to roll this money into an IRA and be charged fees by a wealth manager." And then in an overly sarcastic tone, Ryan said with mounting frustration, "Oh well never mind…it makes perfect sense that they would tell everyone to put as much money into a 401(k) as possible. And who cares about the tax liability this will create for people. That's *their* problem not ours.

And if the client gets double-taxed on their Social Security it doesn't matter because at least Wall Street gets paid." Ryan threw his hands in the air. "And in turn, the financial industry is making money on the client throughout the entire accumulation phase. So, it makes perfect sense that they would tell us to put as much money in the account as possible. Why on earth isn't anybody talking about this?"

"Ryan, we most certainly are talking about this," Mike said, his sober expression matching the expressions on the other men in the room.

After a few more conversations, the meeting came to a close, and Wolf, Josh and Mike walked Ryan to the lobby. When they got to the front doors, Ryan spoke up once again. "I can't believe advisors in the industry have been taking advantage of people for so long."

"I can feel your passion and energy and I get it, Ryan. But we also have a belief here at The IP Group that there are great people and great advisors everywhere. Sometimes it's not the advisor taking advantage of people, but instead, it's the system they are a part of. It's the company, bank, or institution they are part of that sets the rules of the game. We still have faith there are good advisors in bad situations. That said, we will continue to educate as many people as possible so they can make better informed decisions. I certainly hope we are a beacon for any individual, or advisor, that doesn't want to be part of a system they know is flawed." Mike shifted his stance. Mike, Wolf, and Josh shared a nod with each other. "And with that said, the most important question is…do you want to be a part of this?"

With all the conviction he had, Ryan said a confident, "Yes, I do," followed by a series of handshakes with the three men standing across from him. He agreed he would be back early next week to begin the paperwork and process of joining The IP Group.

As Ryan turned to break through the IP doors, Wolf stopped him in his tracks. "Hey, Ryan, are you umpiring this weekend at Minute Maid Park?"

"I am," Ryan said, turning on a heel.

Appendix Eight
A Quick Chart

This chart is a simple reference. The legislation governing these assets is always changing. That said, as a guideline, this chart may help you navigate your future tax liabilities a little better.

The chart illustrates the current tax liability on the withdrawal for certain types of accounts. Also, whether or not the withdrawal from those accounts will add to provisional income, will depend on whether it could lead to taxes on your Social Security. Remember provisional income is a guideline used by the IRS to determine if, and how much of, your Social Security benefit will also be added to your taxable income.

If you would like more of your Social Security benefit, you may aim to keep your provisional income low. If your provisional income is high, you may pay more taxes on a larger portion of your Social Security benefit. Again, this represents the **second** time taxes would be paid on your Social Security.

Account Type/ Name	Taxed at Withdrawal	Provisional Income	Taxed Social Security
401(k)	Yes	Yes	Yes
403(b)	Yes	Yes	Yes
457	Yes	Yes	Yes
Traditional IRA	Yes	Yes	Yes
SEP IRA	Yes	Yes	Yes
Simple IRA	Yes	Yes	Yes
Roth 401(k)	No	No	No
Roth IRA	No	No	No

Chapter Nine

Ninth Inning

It was the bottom of the seventh inning. Minute Maid Park was hosting a college baseball tournament. The score was getting close, and Ryan was behind home plate on high alert. Ready to make an honest umpire call as the pitcher came set, Ryan was crouching low and intensely focused. With a runner on first, one out, and at the top of the order, the home team was positioned to take the lead. Ryan could tell by the sound of the bat that it wasn't going to happen. A hard-hit grounder to short made for an easy double play. The visiting team was out of the inning.

As Ryan brushed off the plate between innings, he caught two familiar faces. Michael James and Wolf were sitting in the first row just off home plate. Making eye contact, Mike heckled, "Hey, Blue, open your eyes."

Ryan, in full umpire mode only smiled and nodded at his future boss as he prepared to get his focus back on the game.

Bolstered with adrenaline knowing his newest role model was watching him, Ryan's focus was piqued for the next two innings. After the patrons in the stands applauded the home team for a 4-3 win, Ryan made his way to where Mike and Wolf were sitting. As Ryan approached, Mike stood up, an emptying stadium behind him dimming the loud noise of the fans from just moments before.

"This is quite the surprise," Ryan said as he reached his hand toward Mike for a handshake greeting while Wolf was heavily engaged in a conversation with a fellow fan.

"I figured I'd come out and see what all the baseball hype was about." Mike passed back a firm grip. "And I gotta say, I'm impressed. I admire your dedication to the sport."

"And I admire your dedication to the financial industry," Ryan said as he motioned for the security guard to open the door that was covered in backstop netting. Mike followed Ryan down to the field, which was filling fast with maintenance workers smoothing the tousled sand and roughed-up grass. Ryan stopped and turned toward Mike. "Umpires are always told to open their eyes, and I gotta tell you...my eyes are open. And for the first time I'm seeing clearer than I ever have before."

"Blue...we're just getting started," Mike said, bumping elbows with Ryan as the two of them approached the dugout. In front of them, the field was already bustling with grooming activity and the players had escaped to the locker rooms, one team celebrating a win, the other sinking in defeat.

Ryan hefted his bag on his shoulder, the weight of his equipment giving him an uneven stance. His eyes were lit with curiosity as he asked, "Mike, can I throw one more question at you?"

"Shoot."

"What does the IP stand for in The IP Group?"

A megawatt, all-knowing smile transformed Mike's face. "The Ideal Portfolio."

The End

Extra Innings

Haven't I been told that pre-tax contributions are better?

If you make a pre-tax 401(k) investment you will be taxed when you make a withdrawal. If you make an after-tax Roth 401(k) investment you will NOT be taxed when you make a withdrawal. If the tax rate at contribution equals the tax rate at withdrawal, the outcome is the same. However, the amount paid in fees to the 401(k) provider is significantly greater on the pre-tax balance. Pre-tax accounts may generate more in revenue for a third party 401(k) plan provider. In this example, I illustrate a pre-tax contribution at $19,000 annually and an after-tax, 15 percent contribution of $16,150. You can see the difference in the amount of fees generated from the balance. All things being equal, the only party earning more on pre-tax dollars in the 401(k) provider.

Traditional 401(k)				
Years	Pre-tax	Return Rate	Balance	Fees 1.25%
1	$19,000	6%	$ 20,140.00	$ 251.75
2	$19,000	6%	$ 41,488.40	$ 518.61
3	$19,000	6%	$ 64,117.70	$ 801.47
4	$19,000	6%	$ 88,104.77	$ 1,101.31
5	$19,000	6%	$ 113,531.05	$ 1,419.14
6	$19,000	6%	$ 140,482.92	$ 1,756.04
7	$19,000	6%	$ 169,051.89	$ 2,113.15
8	$19,000	6%	$ 199,335.00	$ 2,491.69
9	$19,000	6%	$ 231,435.10	$ 2,892.94
10	$19,000	6%	$ 265,461.21	$ 3,318.27
11	$19,000	6%	$ 301,528.88	$ 3,769.11
12	$19,000	6%	$ 339,760.62	$ 4,247.01

Years	Pre-tax	Return Rate	Balance	Fees 1.25%
13	$19,000	6%	$ 380,286.25	$ 4,753.58
14	$19,000	6%	$ 423,243.43	$ 5,290.54
15	$19,000	6%	$ 468,778.03	$ 5,859.73
16	$19,000	6%	$ 517,044.72	$ 6,463.06
17	$19,000	6%	$ 568,207.40	$ 7,102.59
18	$19,000	6%	$ 622,439.84	$ 7,780.50
19	$19,000	6%	$ 679,926.23	$ 8,499.08
20	$19,000	6%	$ 740,861.81	$ 9,260.77
21	$19,000	6%	$ 805,453.52	$ 10,068.17
22	$19,000	6%	$ 873,920.73	$ 10,924.01
23	$19,000	6%	$ 946,495.97	$ 11,831.20
24	$19,000	6%	$ 1,023,425.73	$ 12,792.82
25	$19,000	6%	$ 1,104,971.27	$ 13,812.14
			Total Fees	$139,118.66

Ending Balance	$ 1,104,971.27	
SWR*	3%	
Gross	$ 33,149.14	
Tax Liability	15%	
Net	$ 28,176.77	

Roth 401(k)			
Years	After-Tax 15%	Return Rate	Balance	Fees 1.25%
1	$ 16,150	6%	$ 17,119.00	$ 213.99
2	$ 16,150	6%	$ 35,265.14	$ 440.81
3	$ 16,150	6%	$ 54,500.05	$ 681.25
4	$ 16,150	6%	$ 74,889.05	$ 936.11
5	$ 16,150	6%	$ 96,501.39	$ 1,206.27
6	$ 16,150	6%	$ 119,410.48	$ 1,492.63

Years	After-Tax 15%	Return Rate	Balance	Fees 1.25%
7	$ 16,150	6%	$ 143,694.11	$ 1,796.18
8	$ 16,150	6%	$ 169,434.75	$ 2,117.93
9	$ 16,150	6%	$ 196,719.84	$ 2,459.00
10	$ 16,150	6%	$ 225,642.03	$ 2,820.53
11	$ 16,150	6%	$ 256,299.55	$ 3,203.74
12	$ 16,150	6%	$ 288,796.52	$ 3,609.96
13	$ 16,150	6%	$ 323,243.31	$ 4,040.54
14	$ 16,150	6%	$ 359,756.91	$ 4,496.96
15	$ 16,150	6%	$ 398,461.33	$ 4,980.77
16	$ 16,150	6%	$ 439,488.01	$ 5,493.60
17	$ 16,150	6%	$ 482,976.29	$ 6,037.20
18	$ 16,150	6%	$ 529,073.87	$ 6,613.42
19	$ 16,150	6%	$ 577,937.30	$ 7,224.22
20	$ 16,150	6%	$ 629,732.54	$ 7,871.66
21	$ 16,150	6%	$ 684,635.49	$ 8,557.94
22	$ 16,150	6%	$ 742,832.62	$ 9,285.41
23	$ 16,150	6%	$ 804,521.57	$ 10,056.52
24	$ 16,150	6%	$ 869,911.87	$ 10,873.90
25	$ 16,150	6%	$ 939,225.58	$ 11,740.32
			Total Fees	**$118,250.86**

	Ending Balance	$ 939,225.58	
	SWR*	3%	
	Gross	$ 28,176.77	
	Tax Liability	0%	
	Net	$ 28,176.77	

*SWR stands for safe withdrawal rate. A common assumption used to demonstrate the amount of money it would be "safe" to withdraw annually and not run out of money before mortality.

In this example the tax rates are the same. Ask yourself, will you be in the same tax bracket at age 60, 65, or 70 as you were at age 25, 30, 35?

Strike One: Do you have **Income Potential**? Income Potential is the ability to climb the tax brackets based on ambition, industry, or marriage.

Strike Two: Who is likely to make more money if you defer your taxes?

Strike Three: Do you believe taxes will increase or decrease in the future?

Pre-tax 401(k), you're out!

If you enjoyed this book, please leave a review on Amazon so other readers can learn the truth about tax liability. Also, you can stay updated on an endless supply of information by checking out www.ballsandstrikesbook.com.

Next up in the series, is Heels and Deals. Join Taylor Roth as she learns the hard truth about income potential and the vast differences surrounding today's retirement options. *This is no longer your parent's retirement.* When Taylor sets out to get her annual taxes done, she expects the appointment to be no different than those in the past. She'll hand over her tax documents, fill out a few forms and file away. But when she meets Accountant, Maggie Dean, she discovers that she has a lot to learn about saving for the future.

Taylor's father, Jim Roth, is a well-known leader in the finance arena, who has spent his life driving the message that the Big Broker Companies have instilled in him for decades. Taylor quickly learns that the dad she admires has been spreading a deeply disturbing message to employees and investors across the heart of Houston. With the help of the cast from Balls and Strikes, Taylor challenges her father's knowledge, and the heat is on as Maggie, Ryan, Michael James, and a few new faces, dissect the common misconceptions that Wall Street has been spreading about saving for the future.

Acknowledgments

I would like to thank so many people. I truly believe I have a lot to give because so many have given to me. Colleagues, friends, and family in St. Louis, Chicago, Santa Monica, Los Angeles, and Houston have all impacted my journey.

Kate, you know what's up. This book(s), see what I did there, wouldn't get done without you. I lost track of how many words you and I have accidently created. Thank you for helping with my exclamation point problem......! Damn it...!!

Our leadership team: Blue, Mo, Red, Alex, and TMac, thank you for continuing to challenge me and hold me accountable. Thank you for allowing me to challenge all of you. You all know I believe there is nothing we can't accomplish.

I would also like to acknowledge the following authors who continue to inspire me. These authors and their audiobooks have replaced my workout playlist. Kate Anslinger, Ann Hiatt, Ray Dalio, David Goggins, Eric Ries, Brene Brown, Walter Isaacson, Tim Grover, Ben Newman, and Bryan Bloom. Thank you all for sharing your passion.

The Wolf and Mr. Anderson, your belief in our message has started a movement... we are not done yet. Thank you for A LOT.

Bibliography

Brandon, Emily. "Are Your Retirement Savings Ahead of the Curve?" US News & World Report. November 2020. Accessed May 12, 2021. https://money.usnews.com/money/retirement/401ks/articles/are-your-retirement-savings-ahead-of-the-curve.

Olshan, Jeremy. "The Inventor of the 401(k) says he created a 'monster.'" Market Watch, September 2016. Accessed May 5, 2021, https://www.marketwatch.com/story/the-inventor-of-the-401k-says-he-created-a-monster-2016-05-16.

https://www.irs.gov/statistics/soi-tax-stats-individual-tax-statistics

DQYDJ, Calculators and Tools, accessed July 30, 2021, https://dqydj.com/calculators/

History of Federal Income Tax Rates: 1913 – 2021. Accessed August 1, 2021. https://bradfordtaxinstitute.com.

Benz, Christine. "Retirees: Are You Spending Too Much?" Morningstar. January 2021. Accessed August 2, 2021, https://www.morningstar.com/articles/844210/retirees-are-you-spending-too-much

Pension Right Center. April 16, 2021. Accessed August 3, 2021. https://www.pensionrights.org/publications/statistic/income-today%E2%80%99s-older-adults

About the Author

Tehrrek would say he is not special; he simply owns a calculator. Having been in the financial services industry for seventeen years, he has witnessed a lot and has discovered that challenging the status quo is his passion. After he received his degree in economics from the University of Illinois at Urbana Champaign, he worked in St. Louis, Los Angeles, Santa Monica, Chicago, and Houston. His vast experience had led him to believe that people everywhere generally share his concern that the financial services industry has gone astray. While he believes that there are still great people in this field, he suggests the industry itself has transpired into one that is more focused on making money than on helping individuals. Above all else, he is passionate about creating The Ideal Portfolio and helping people utilize the portfolio to their advantage. Tehrrek lives in Houston, Texas where he continues to educate and assist as many people as possible. He hopes you'll join him on his mission to finding a better way.

To learn more, go to: www.ballsandstrikesbook.com